D0500044

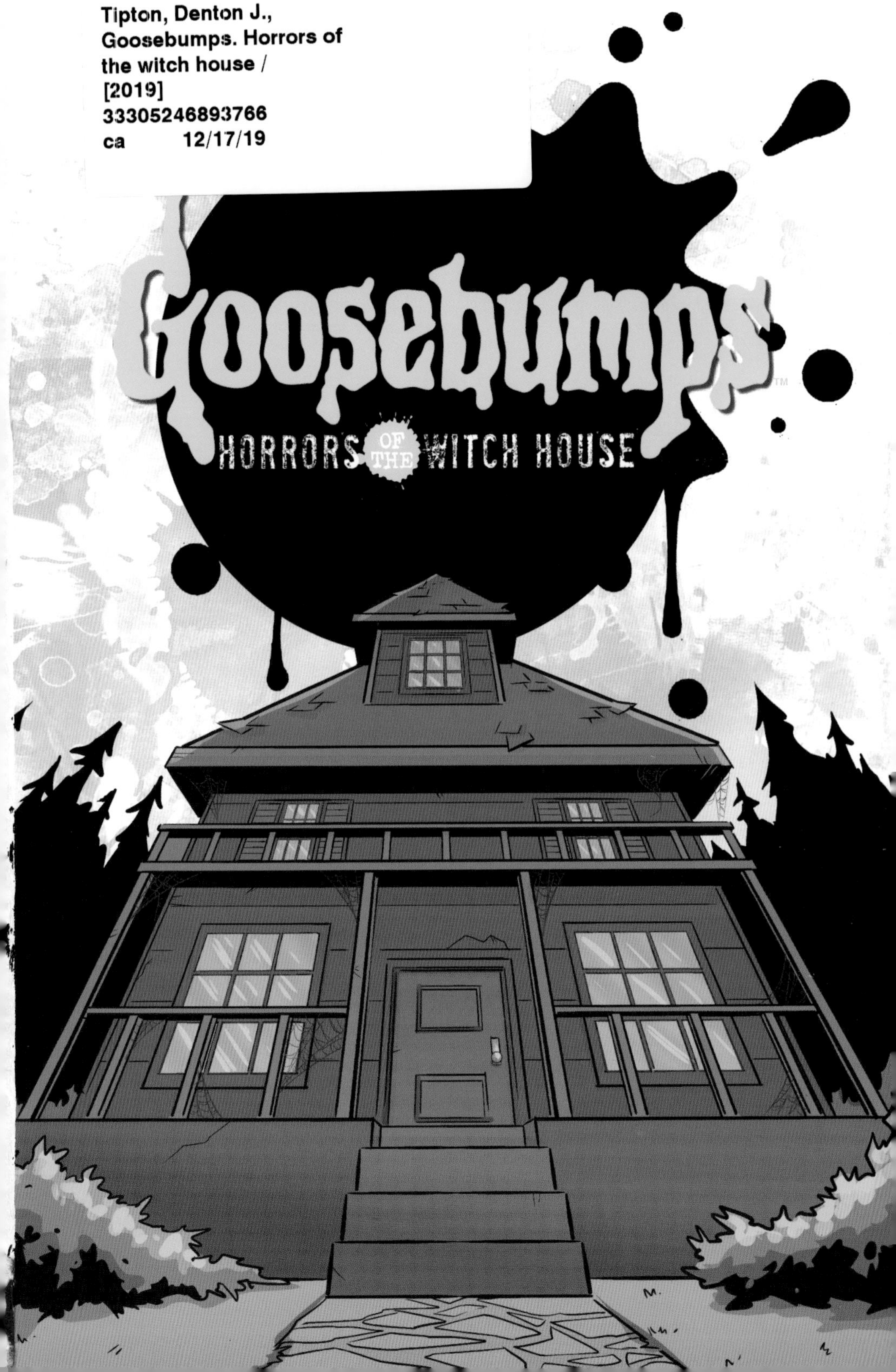
Goosebumps™
HORRORS OF THE WITCH HOUSE

Become our fan on Facebook **facebook.com/idwpublishing**
Follow us on Twitter **@idwpublishing**
Subscribe to us on YouTube **youtube.com/idwpublishing**
See what's new on Tumblr **tumblr.idwpublishing.com**
Check us out on Instagram **instagram.com/idwpublishing**

www.IDWPUBLISHING.com

Chris Ryall, President, Publisher, & CCO
John Barber, Editor-In-Chief
Cara Morrison, Chief Financial Officer
Matt Ruzicka, Chief Accounting Officer
David Hedgecock, Associate Publisher
Jerry Bennington, VP of New Product Development
Lorelei Bunjes, VP of Digital Services
Justin Eisinger, Editorial Director, Graphic Novels & Collections
Eric Moss, Senior Director, Licensing and Business Development

Ted Adams and Robbie Robbins, IDW Founders

ISBN: 978-1-68405-539-5   22 21 20 19   1 2 3 4

COVER ARTIST
CHRIS FENOGLIO

SERIES EDITORIAL ASSISTANT
ANNI PERHEENTUPA

SERIES ASSISTANT EDITOR
ELIZABETH BREI

SERIES EDITOR
CHASE MAROTZ

COLLECTION EDITORS
JUSTIN EISINGER
AND ALONZO SIMON

COLLECTION DESIGNER
CLAUDIA CHONG

Originally published as GOOSEBUMPS: HORRORS OF THE WITCH HOUSE issues #1–3.

Special thanks to R.L. Stine.

For international rights, contact licensing@idwpublishing.com

SCHOLASTIC

Goosebumps

HORRORS OF THE WITCH HOUSE

WRITTEN BY
**DENTON J. TIPTON
& MATTHEW DOW SMITH**

ART BY
CHRIS FENOGLIO

COLORS BY
VALENTINA PINTO

LETTERS BY
CHRISTA MIESNER

ART BY **CHRIS FENOGLIO**

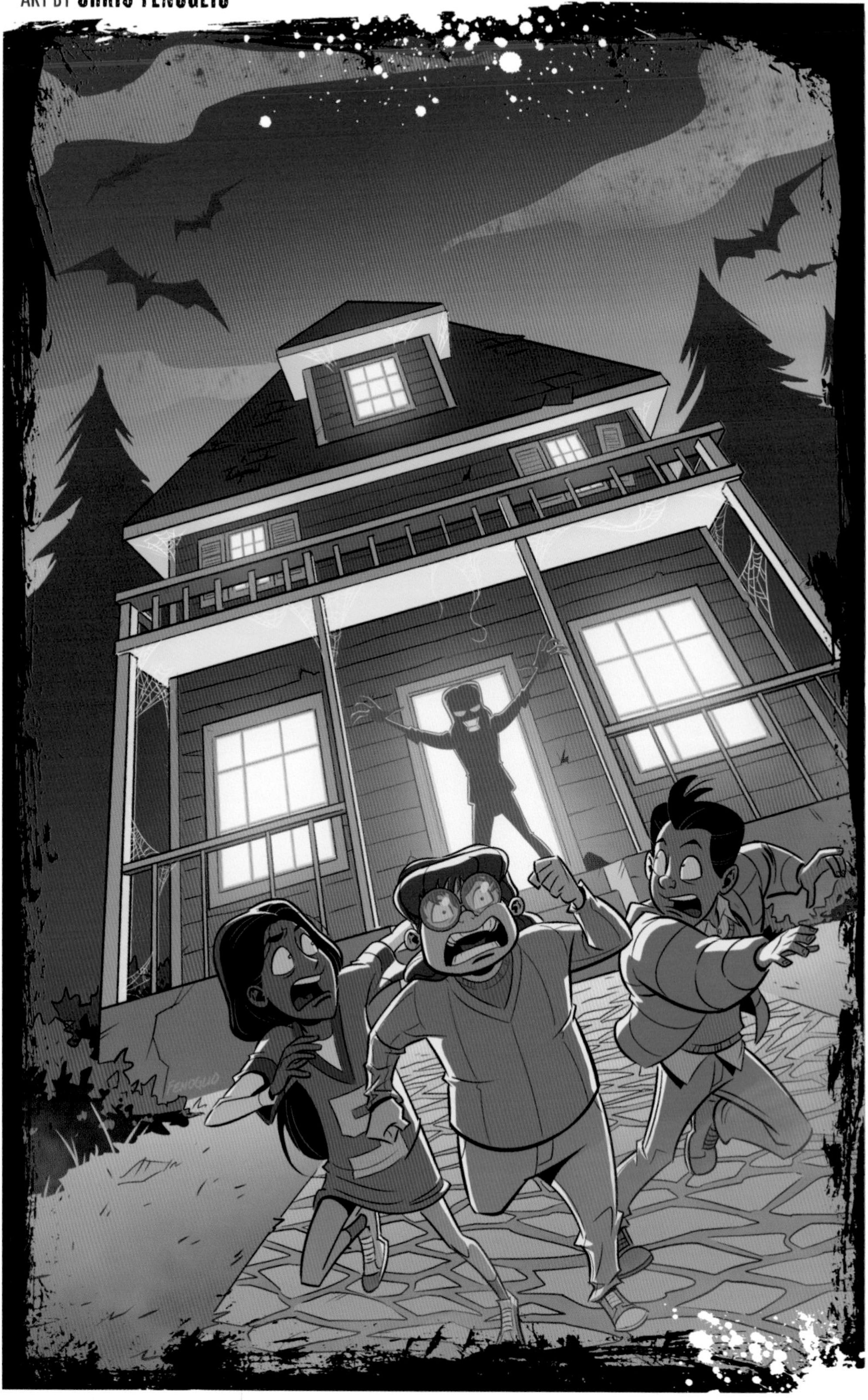

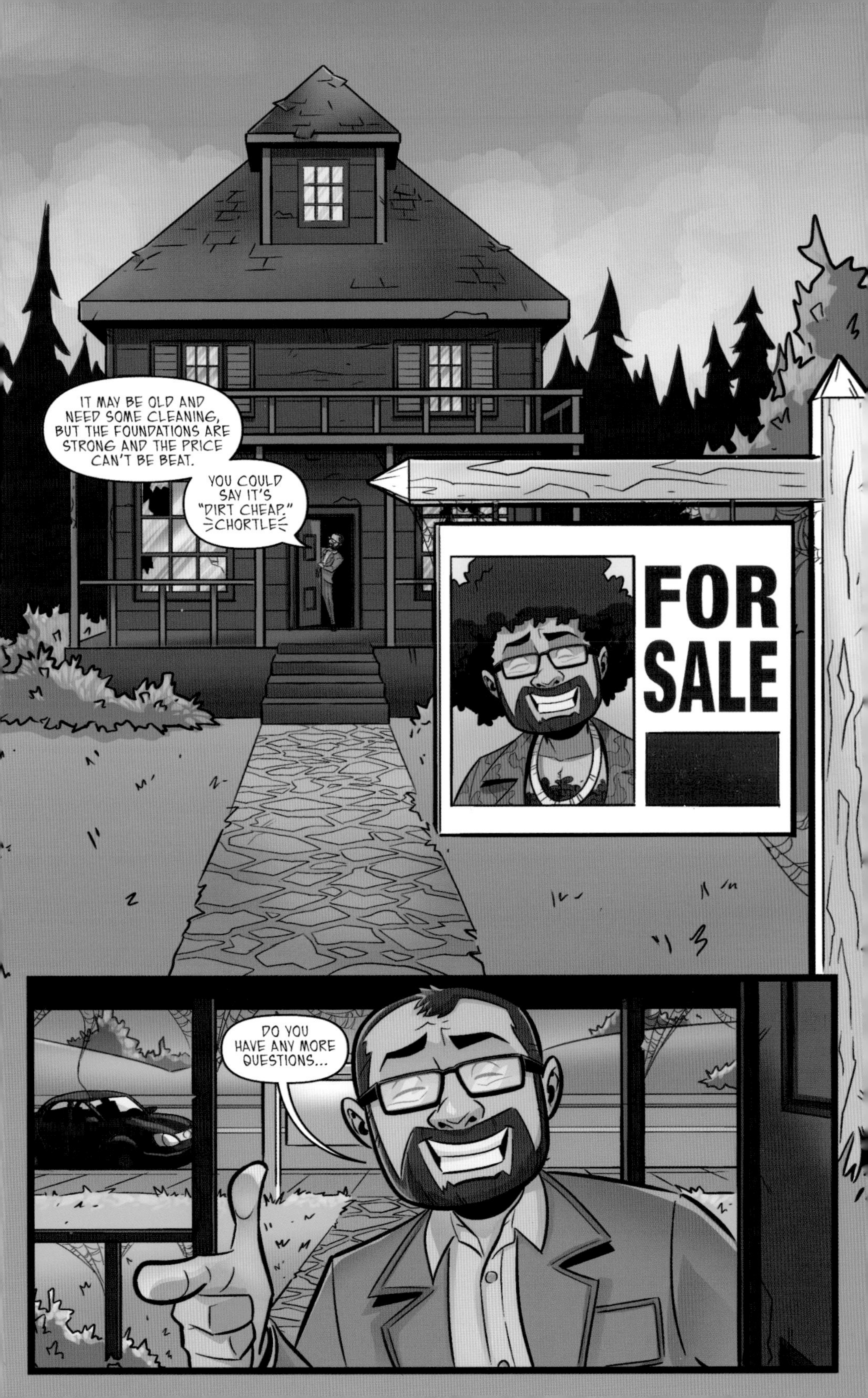
IT MAY BE OLD AND NEED SOME CLEANING, BUT THE FOUNDATIONS ARE STRONG AND THE PRICE CAN'T BE BEAT.
YOU COULD SAY IT'S "DIRT CHEAP." CHORTLE
FOR SALE
DO YOU HAVE ANY MORE QUESTIONS...

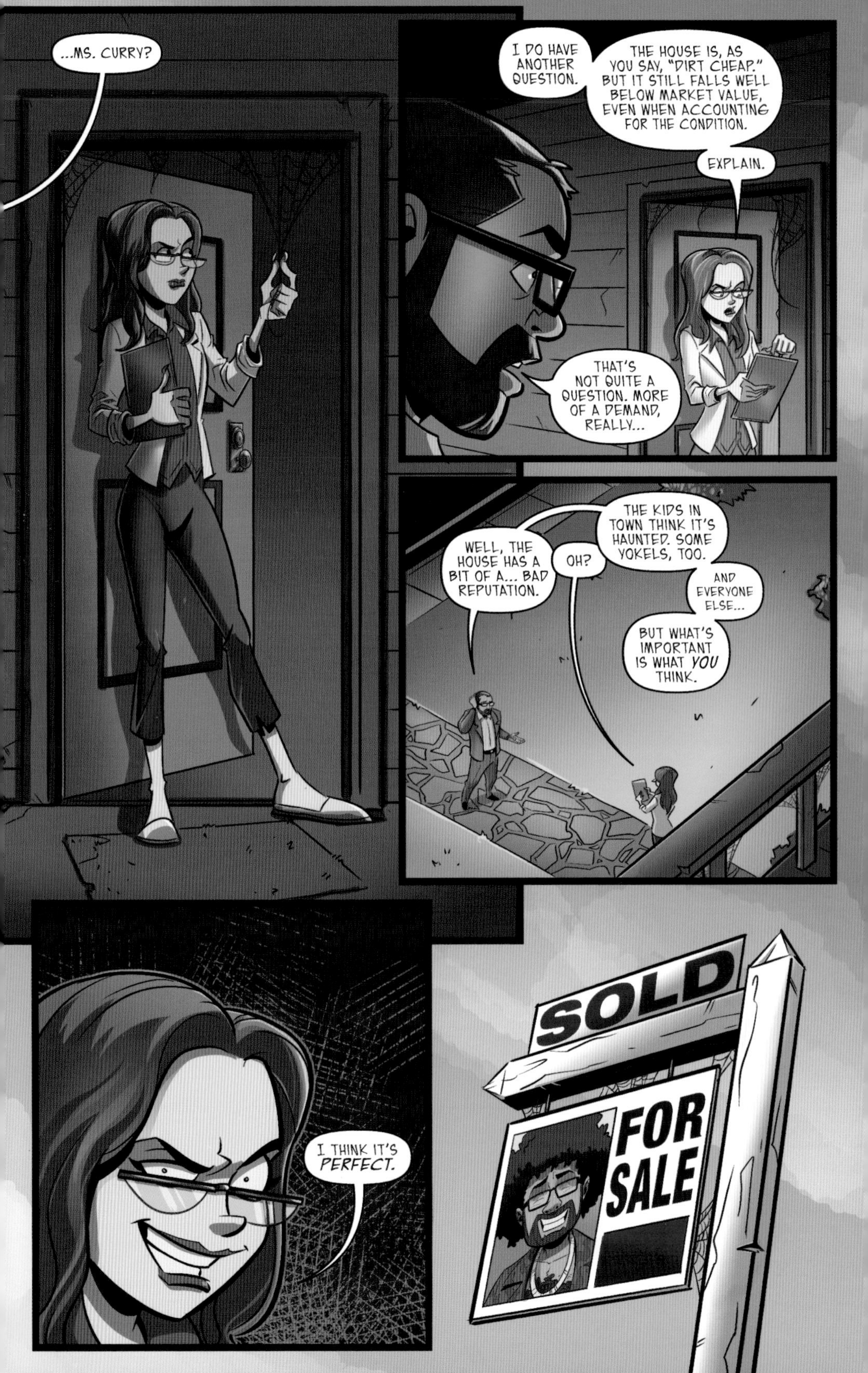
...MS. CURRY?
I DO HAVE ANOTHER QUESTION.
THE HOUSE IS, AS YOU SAY, "DIRT CHEAP." BUT IT STILL FALLS WELL BELOW MARKET VALUE, EVEN WHEN ACCOUNTING FOR THE CONDITION.
EXPLAIN.
THAT'S NOT QUITE A QUESTION. MORE OF A DEMAND, REALLY...
WELL, THE HOUSE HAS A BIT OF A... BAD REPUTATION.
OH?
THE KIDS IN TOWN THINK IT'S HAUNTED. SOME YOKELS, TOO.
AND EVERYONE ELSE...
BUT WHAT'S IMPORTANT IS WHAT *YOU* THINK.
I THINK IT'S *PERFECT.*
SOLD
FOR SALE

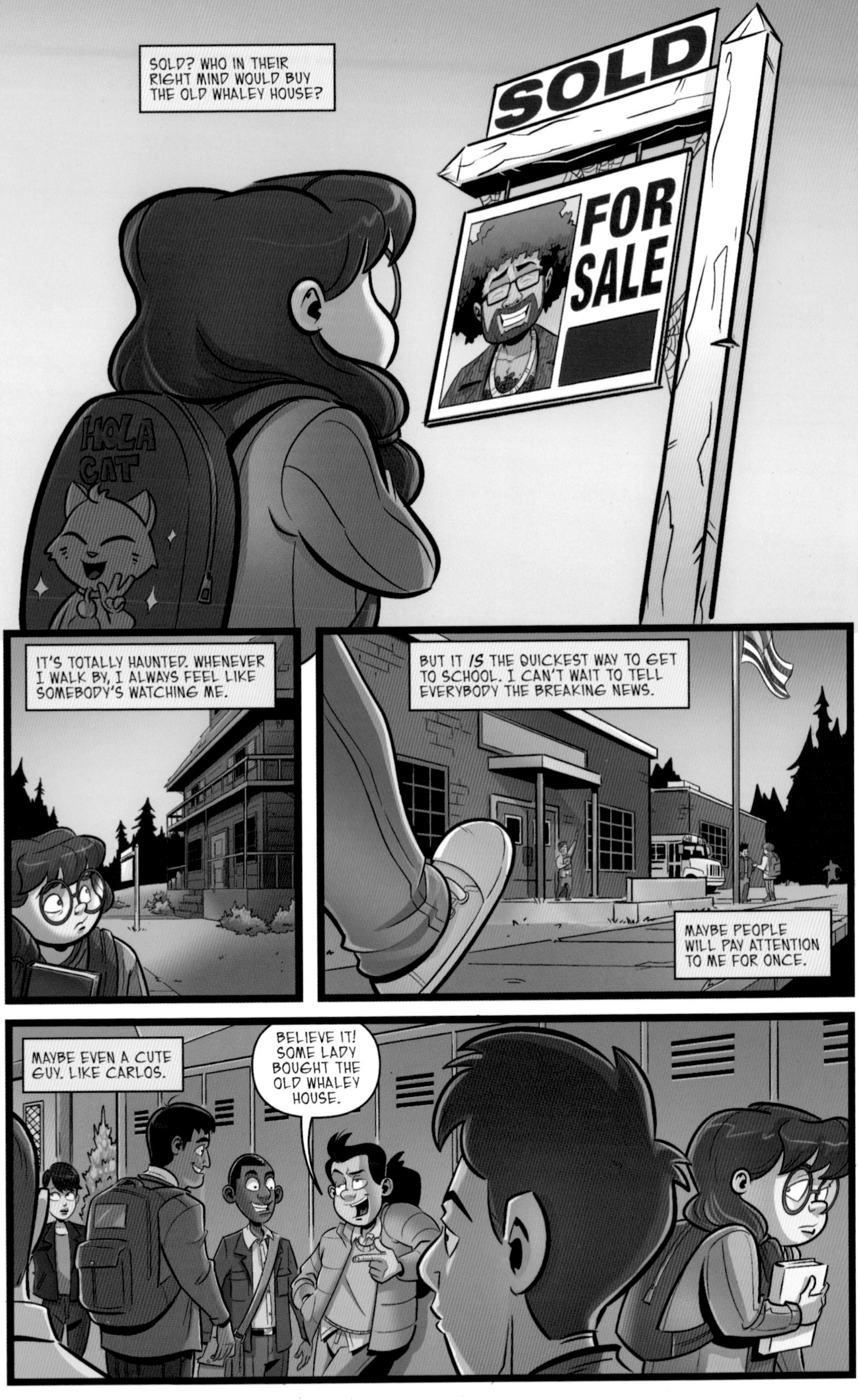
SOLD? WHO IN THEIR RIGHT MIND WOULD BUY THE OLD WHALEY HOUSE?
SOLD
FOR SALE
HOLA CAT
IT'S TOTALLY HAUNTED. WHENEVER I WALK BY, I ALWAYS FEEL LIKE SOMEBODY'S WATCHING ME.
BUT IT IS THE QUICKEST WAY TO GET TO SCHOOL. I CAN'T WAIT TO TELL EVERYBODY THE BREAKING NEWS.
MAYBE PEOPLE WILL PAY ATTENTION TO ME FOR ONCE.
MAYBE EVEN A CUTE GUY. LIKE CARLOS.
BELIEVE IT! SOME LADY BOUGHT THE OLD WHALEY HOUSE.

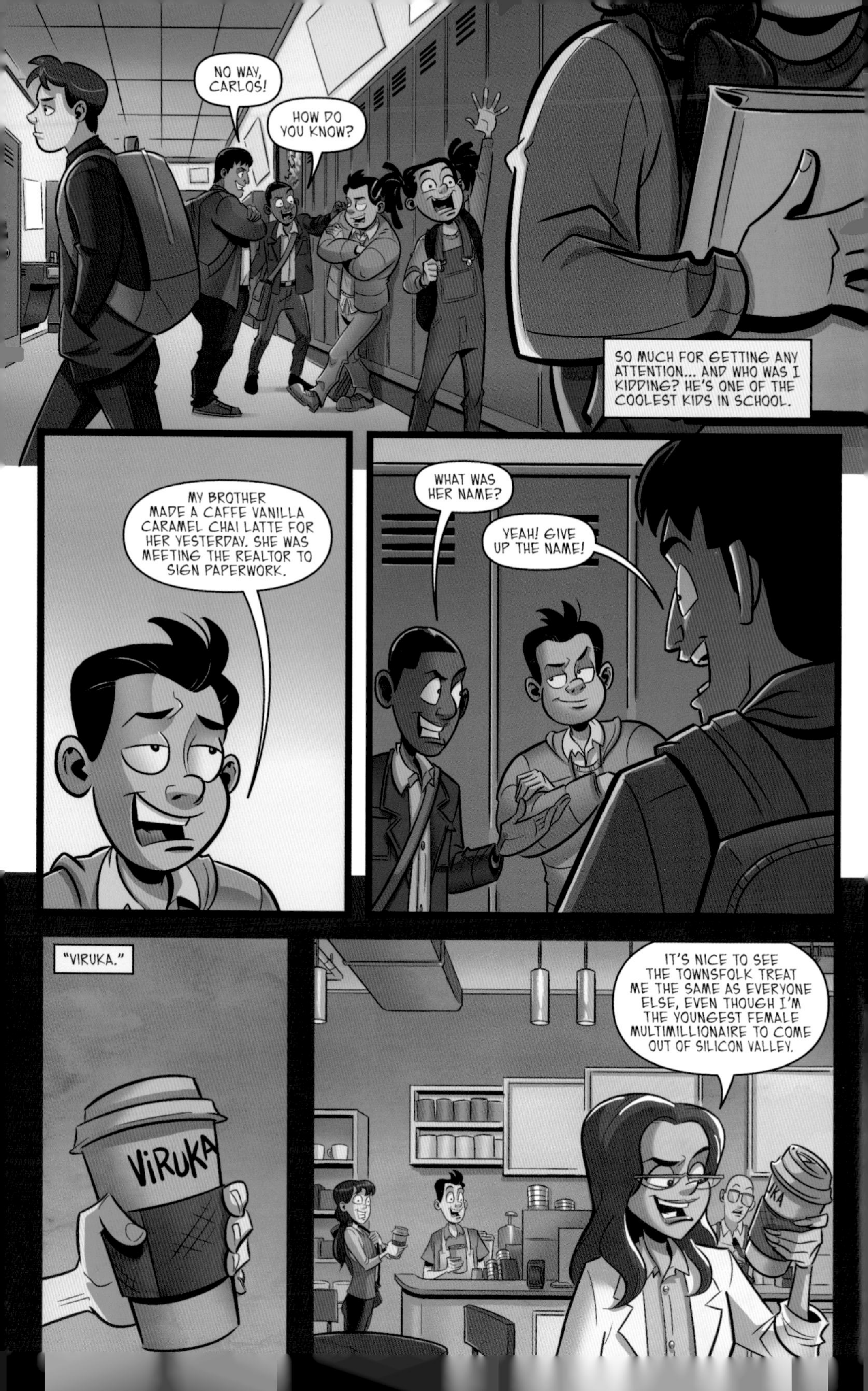
NO WAY, CARLOS!
HOW DO YOU KNOW?
SO MUCH FOR GETTING ANY ATTENTION... AND WHO WAS I KIDDING? HE'S ONE OF THE COOLEST KIDS IN SCHOOL.
MY BROTHER MADE A CAFFE VANILLA CARAMEL CHAI LATTE FOR HER YESTERDAY. SHE WAS MEETING THE REALTOR TO SIGN PAPERWORK.
WHAT WAS HER NAME?
YEAH! GIVE UP THE NAME!
"VIRUKA."
VIRUKA
IT'S NICE TO SEE THE TOWNSFOLK TREAT ME THE SAME AS EVERYONE ELSE, EVEN THOUGH I'M THE YOUNGEST FEMALE MULTIMILLIONAIRE TO COME OUT OF SILICON VALLEY.

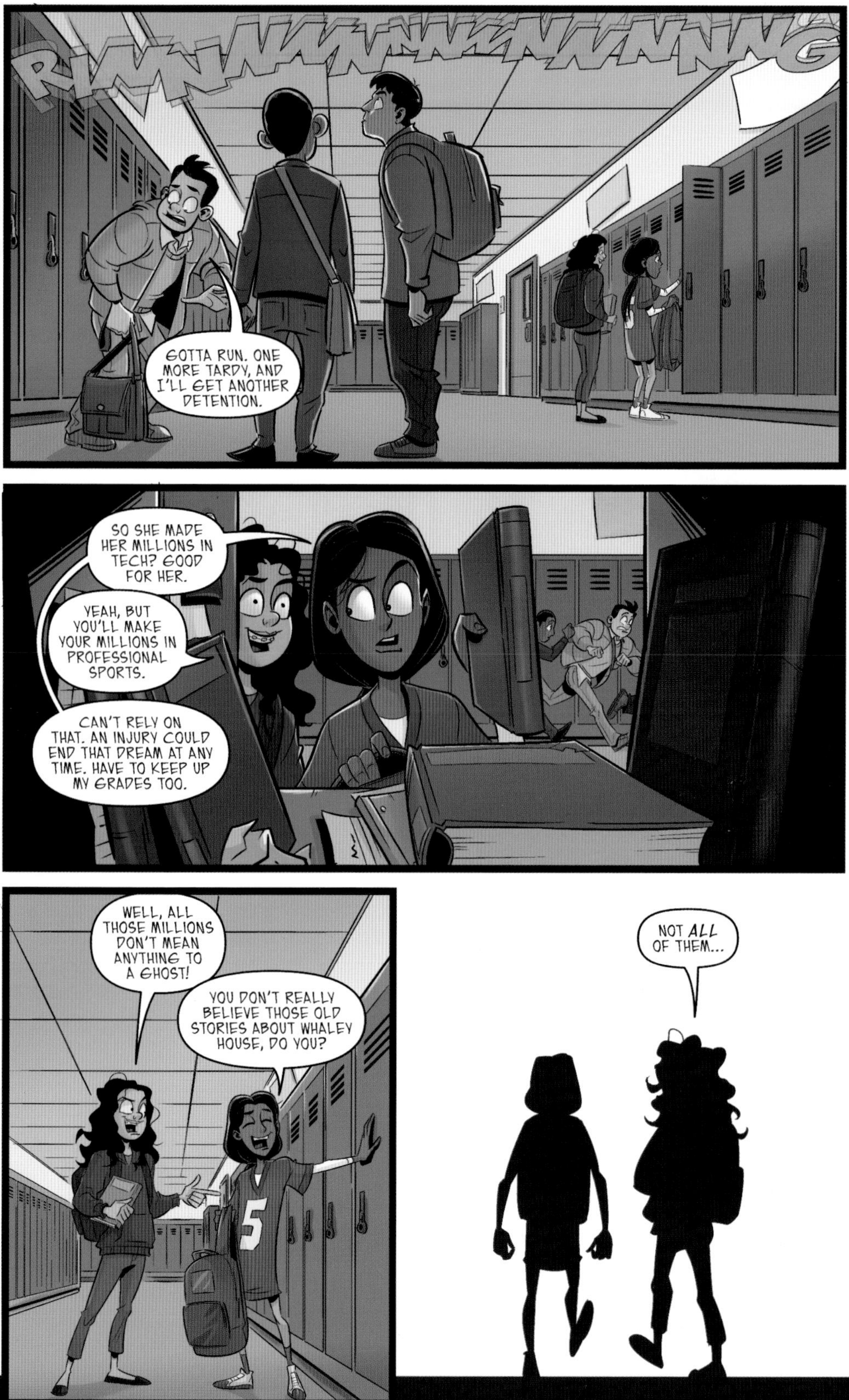
RIIIIINNNNNNNNNNNNNNNNNG
GOTTA RUN. ONE MORE TARDY, AND I'LL GET ANOTHER DETENTION.
SO SHE MADE HER MILLIONS IN TECH? GOOD FOR HER.
YEAH, BUT YOU'LL MAKE YOUR MILLIONS IN PROFESSIONAL SPORTS.
CAN'T RELY ON THAT. AN INJURY COULD END THAT DREAM AT ANY TIME. HAVE TO KEEP UP MY GRADES TOO.
WELL, ALL THOSE MILLIONS DON'T MEAN ANYTHING TO A GHOST!
YOU DON'T REALLY BELIEVE THOSE OLD STORIES ABOUT WHALEY HOUSE, DO YOU?
NOT *ALL* OF THEM...

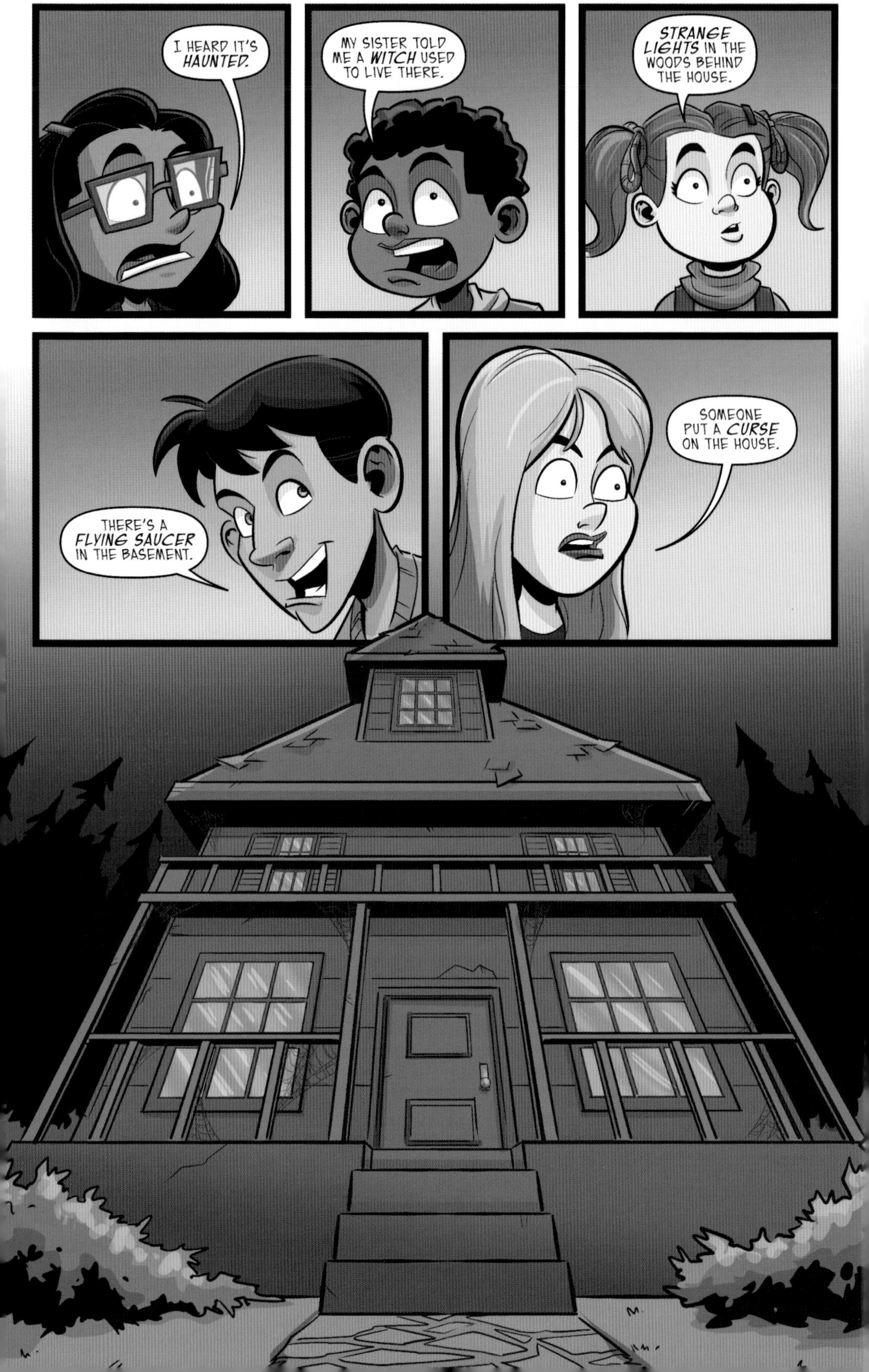
I HEARD IT'S HAUNTED.
MY SISTER TOLD ME A WITCH USED TO LIVE THERE.
STRANGE LIGHTS IN THE WOODS BEHIND THE HOUSE.
THERE'S A FLYING SAUCER IN THE BASEMENT.
SOMEONE PUT A CURSE ON THE HOUSE.

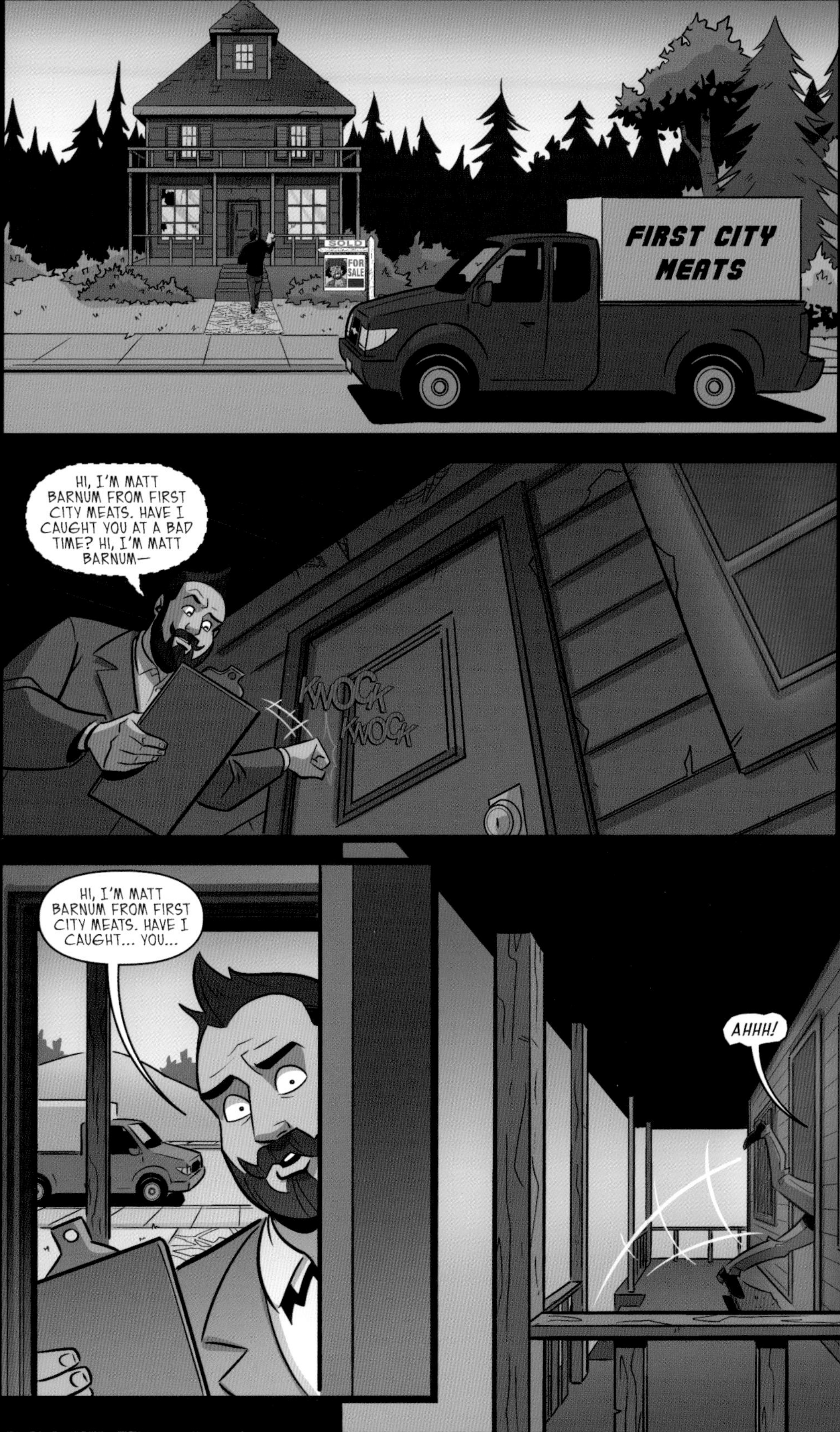
SOLD
FOR SALE
FIRST CITY MEATS
HI, I'M MATT BARNUM FROM FIRST CITY MEATS. HAVE I CAUGHT YOU AT A BAD TIME? HI, I'M MATT BARNUM—
KNOCK KNOCK
HI, I'M MATT BARNUM FROM FIRST CITY MEATS. HAVE I CAUGHT... YOU...
AHHH!

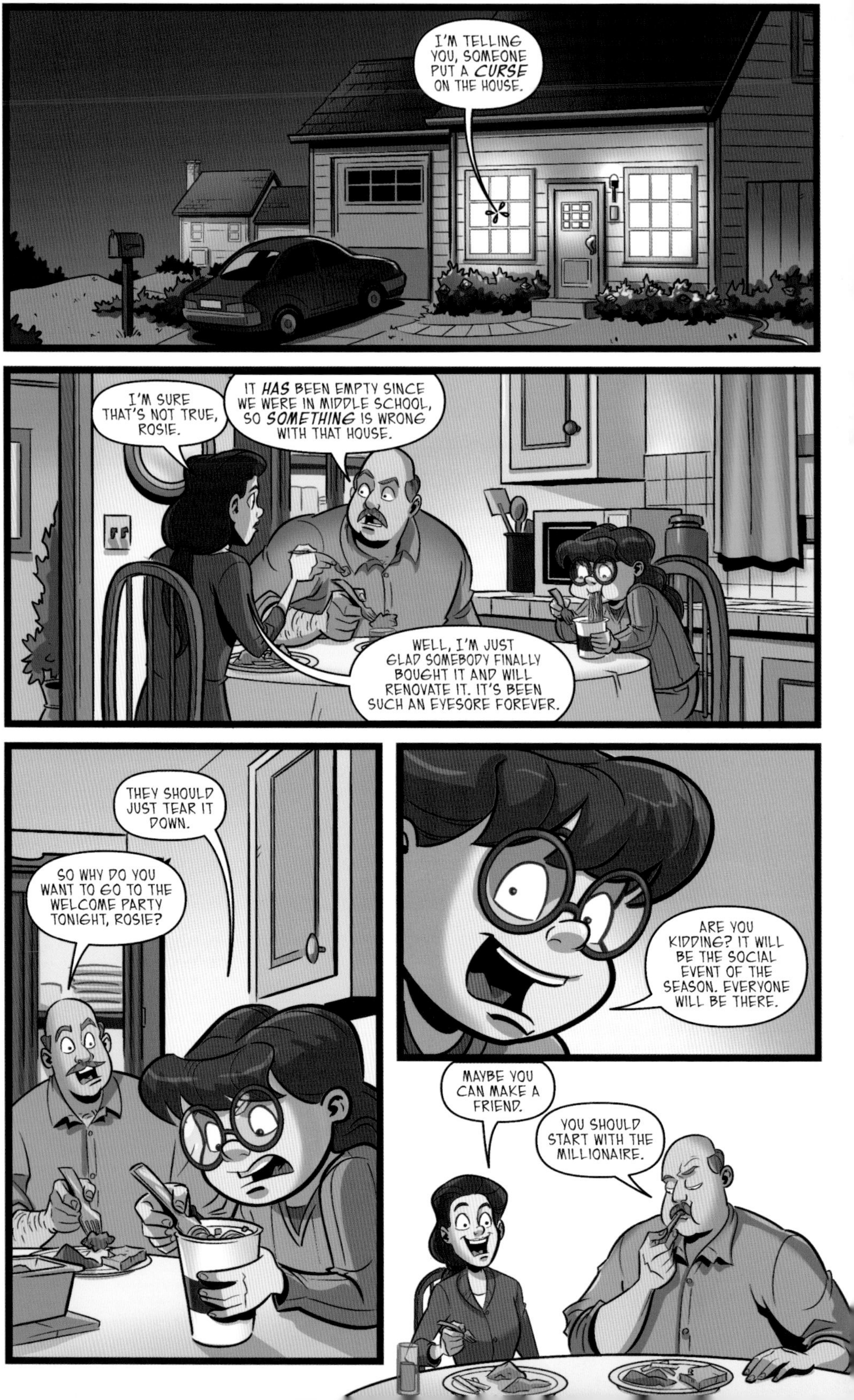
I'M TELLING YOU, SOMEONE PUT A CURSE ON THE HOUSE.
I'M SURE THAT'S NOT TRUE, ROSIE.
IT HAS BEEN EMPTY SINCE WE WERE IN MIDDLE SCHOOL, SO SOMETHING IS WRONG WITH THAT HOUSE.
WELL, I'M JUST GLAD SOMEBODY FINALLY BOUGHT IT AND WILL RENOVATE IT. IT'S BEEN SUCH AN EYESORE FOREVER.
THEY SHOULD JUST TEAR IT DOWN.
SO WHY DO YOU WANT TO GO TO THE WELCOME PARTY TONIGHT, ROSIE?
ARE YOU KIDDING? IT WILL BE THE SOCIAL EVENT OF THE SEASON. EVERYONE WILL BE THERE.
MAYBE YOU CAN MAKE A FRIEND.
YOU SHOULD START WITH THE MILLIONAIRE.

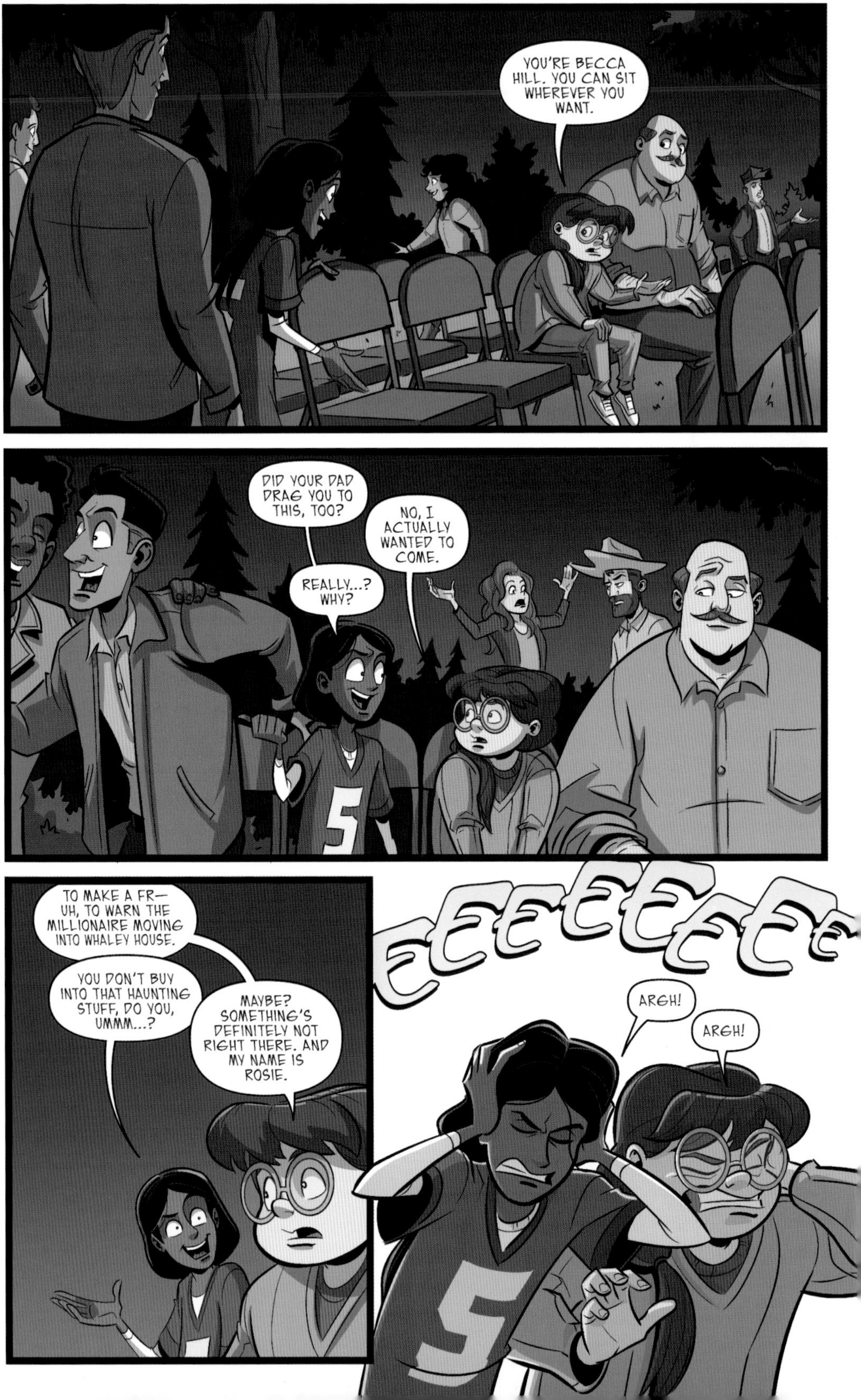
YOU'RE BECCA HILL. YOU CAN SIT WHEREVER YOU WANT.
DID YOUR DAD DRAG YOU TO THIS, TOO?
NO, I ACTUALLY WANTED TO COME.
REALLY...? WHY?
TO MAKE A FR— UH, TO WARN THE MILLIONAIRE MOVING INTO WHALEY HOUSE.
YOU DON'T BUY INTO THAT HAUNTING STUFF, DO YOU, UMMM...?
MAYBE? SOMETHING'S DEFINITELY NOT RIGHT THERE. AND MY NAME IS ROSIE.
EEEEEEEEEE
ARGH!
ARGH!

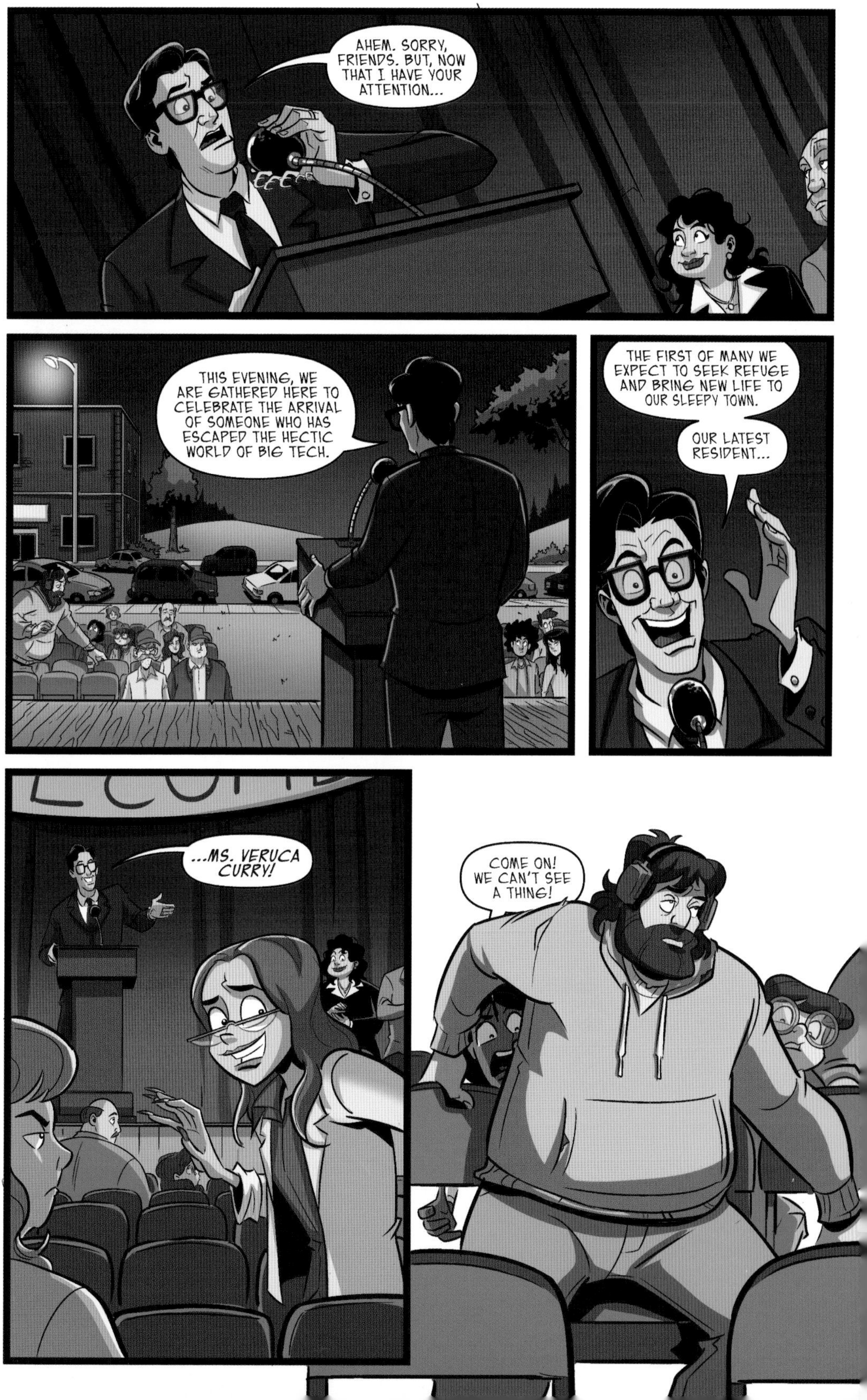
AHEM. SORRY, FRIENDS. BUT, NOW THAT I HAVE YOUR ATTENTION...
EEEEE
THIS EVENING, WE ARE GATHERED HERE TO CELEBRATE THE ARRIVAL OF SOMEONE WHO HAS ESCAPED THE HECTIC WORLD OF BIG TECH.
THE FIRST OF MANY WE EXPECT TO SEEK REFUGE AND BRING NEW LIFE TO OUR SLEEPY TOWN.
OUR LATEST RESIDENT...
...MS. VERUCA CURRY!
COME ON! WE CAN'T SEE A THING!

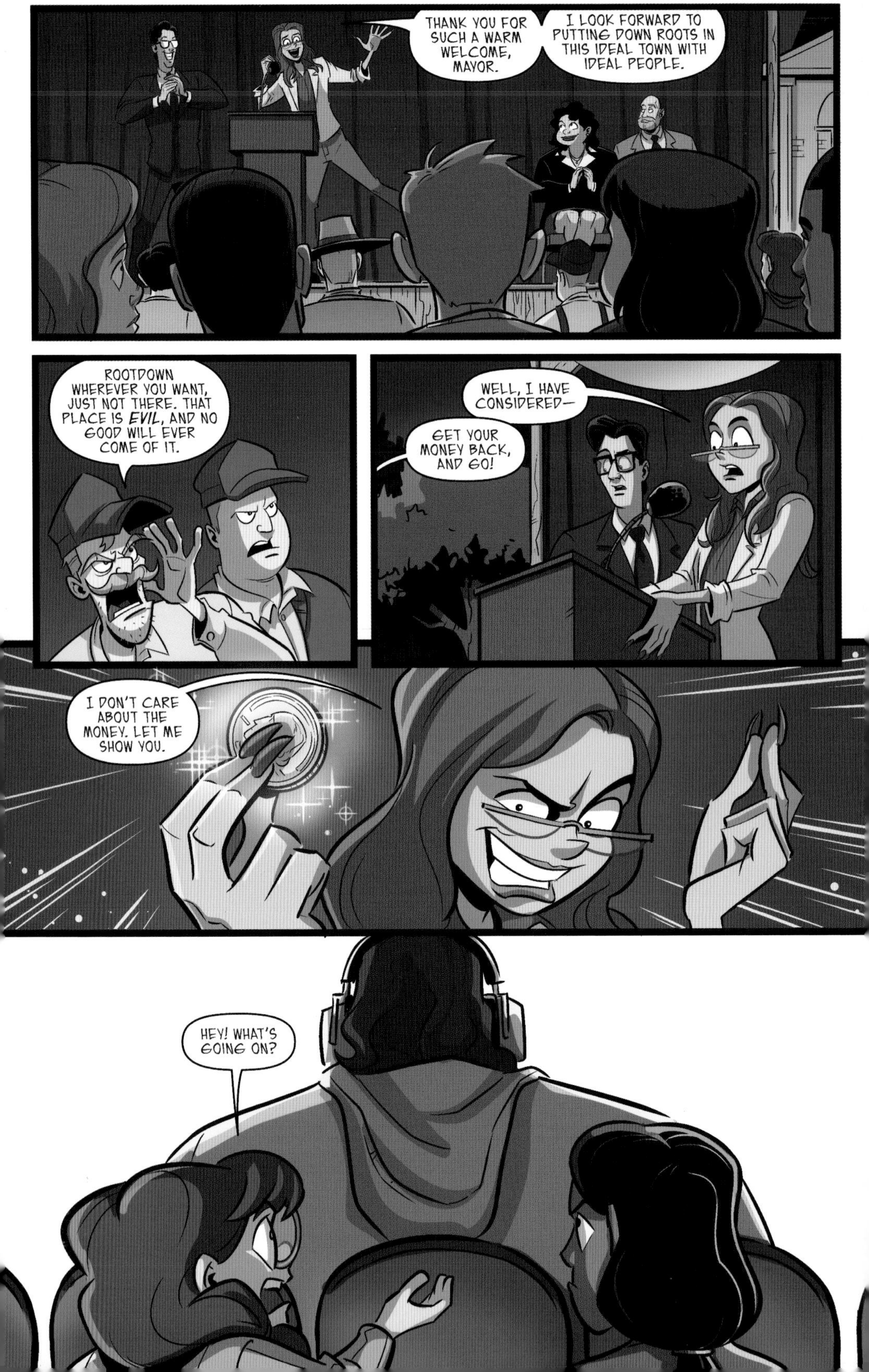

THANK YOU FOR SUCH A WARM WELCOME, MAYOR.
I LOOK FORWARD TO PUTTING DOWN ROOTS IN THIS IDEAL TOWN WITH IDEAL PEOPLE.
ROOTDOWN WHEREVER YOU WANT, JUST NOT THERE. THAT PLACE IS *EVIL*, AND NO GOOD WILL EVER COME OF IT.
WELL, I HAVE CONSIDERED—
GET YOUR MONEY BACK, AND GO!
I DON'T CARE ABOUT THE MONEY. LET ME SHOW YOU.
HEY! WHAT'S GOING ON?

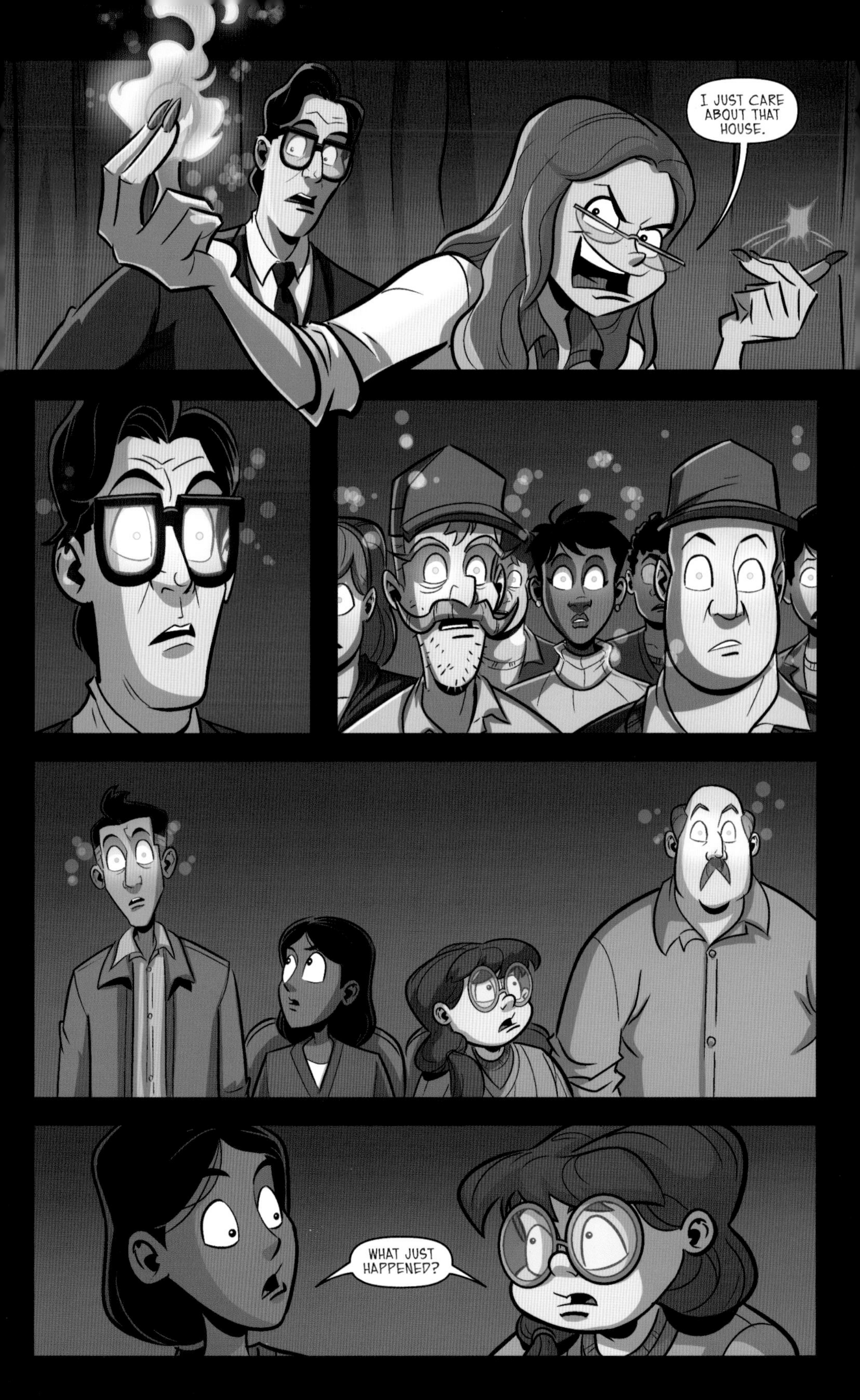
I JUST CARE ABOUT THAT HOUSE.
WHAT JUST HAPPENED?

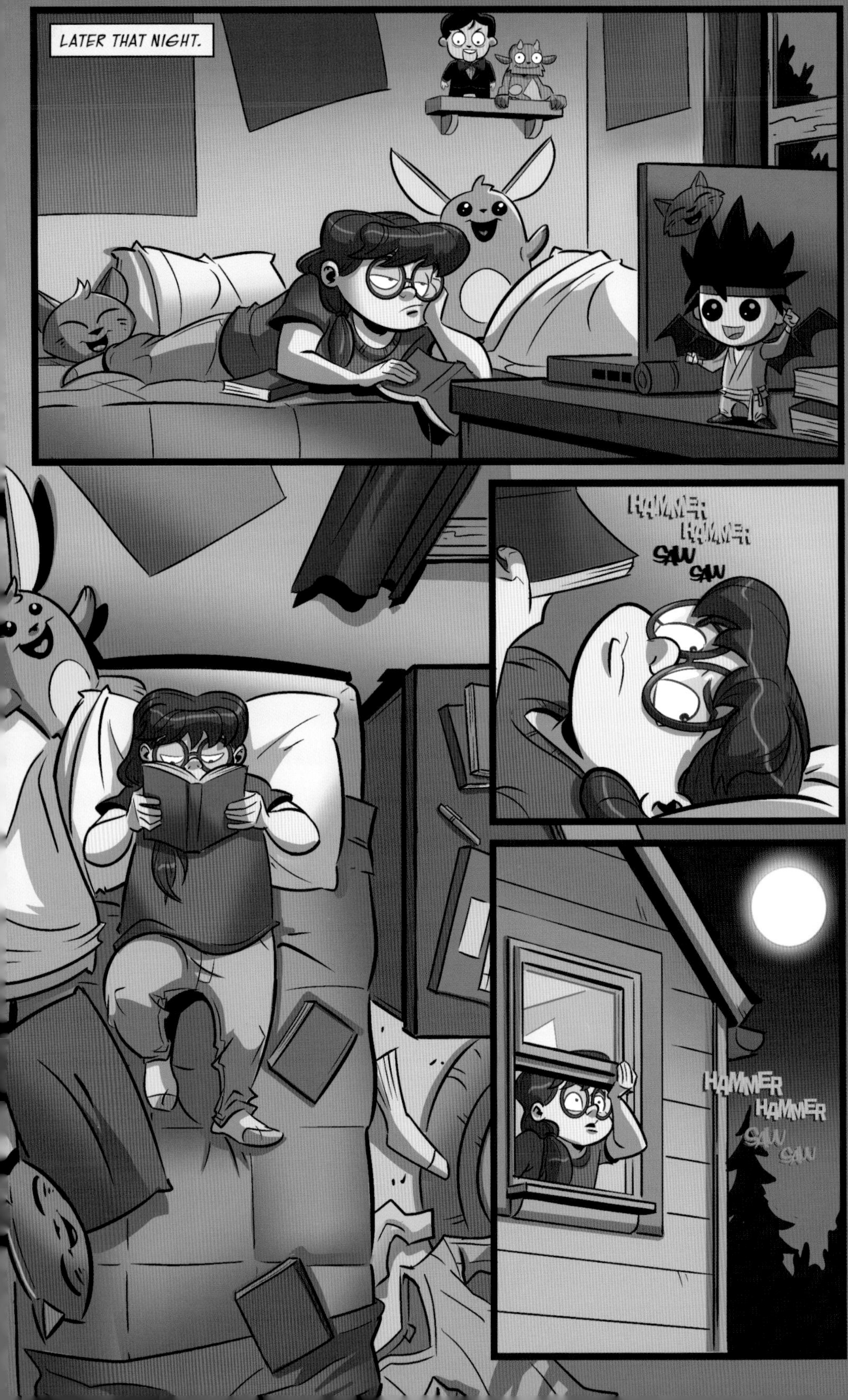
LATER THAT NIGHT.
HAMMER
HAMMER
SAW
SAW
HAMMER
HAMMER
SAW
SAW

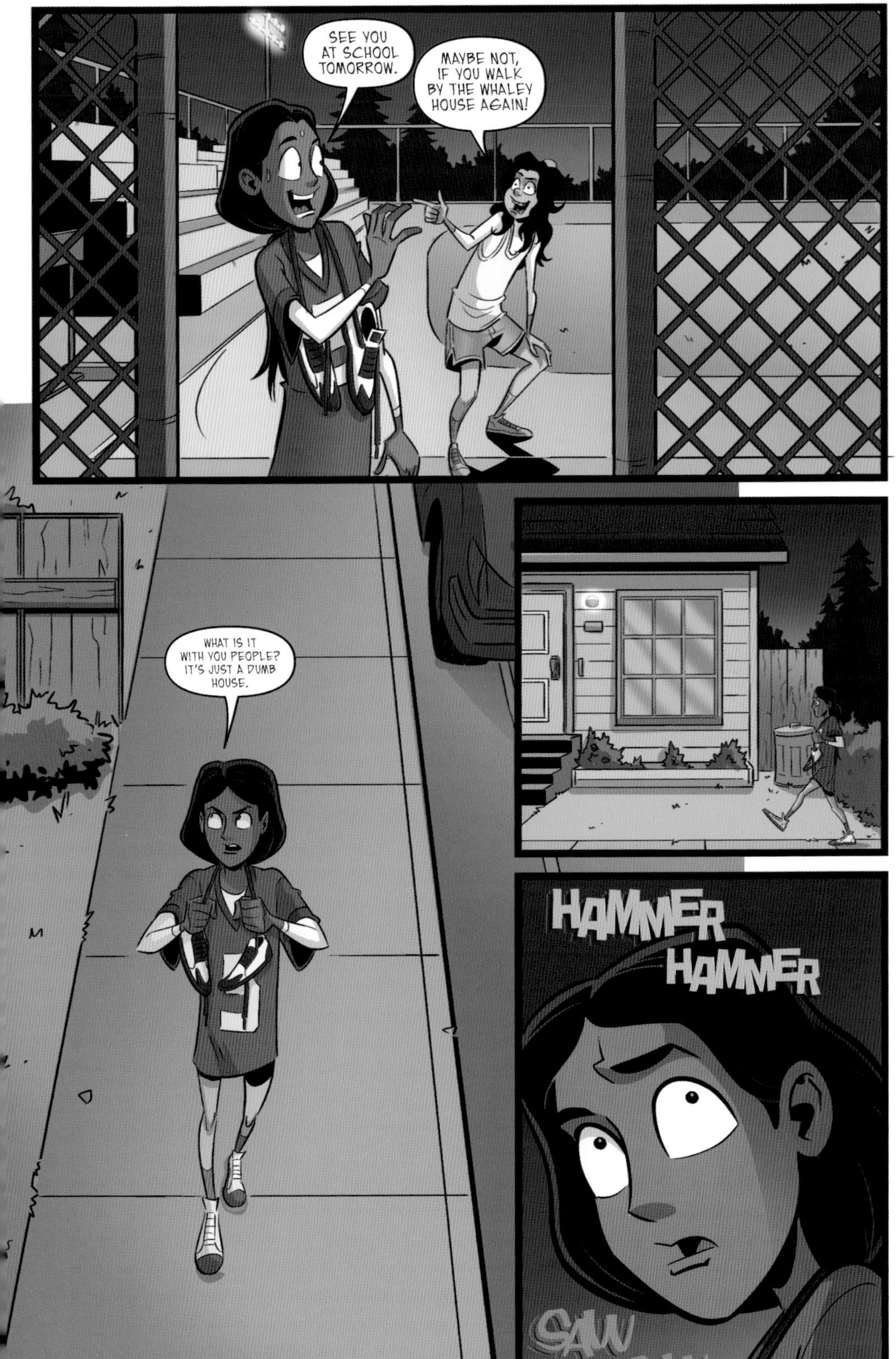
SEE YOU AT SCHOOL TOMORROW.
MAYBE NOT, IF YOU WALK BY THE WHALEY HOUSE AGAIN!
WHAT IS IT WITH YOU PEOPLE? IT'S JUST A DUMB HOUSE.
HAMMER
HAMMER
SAW
SAW

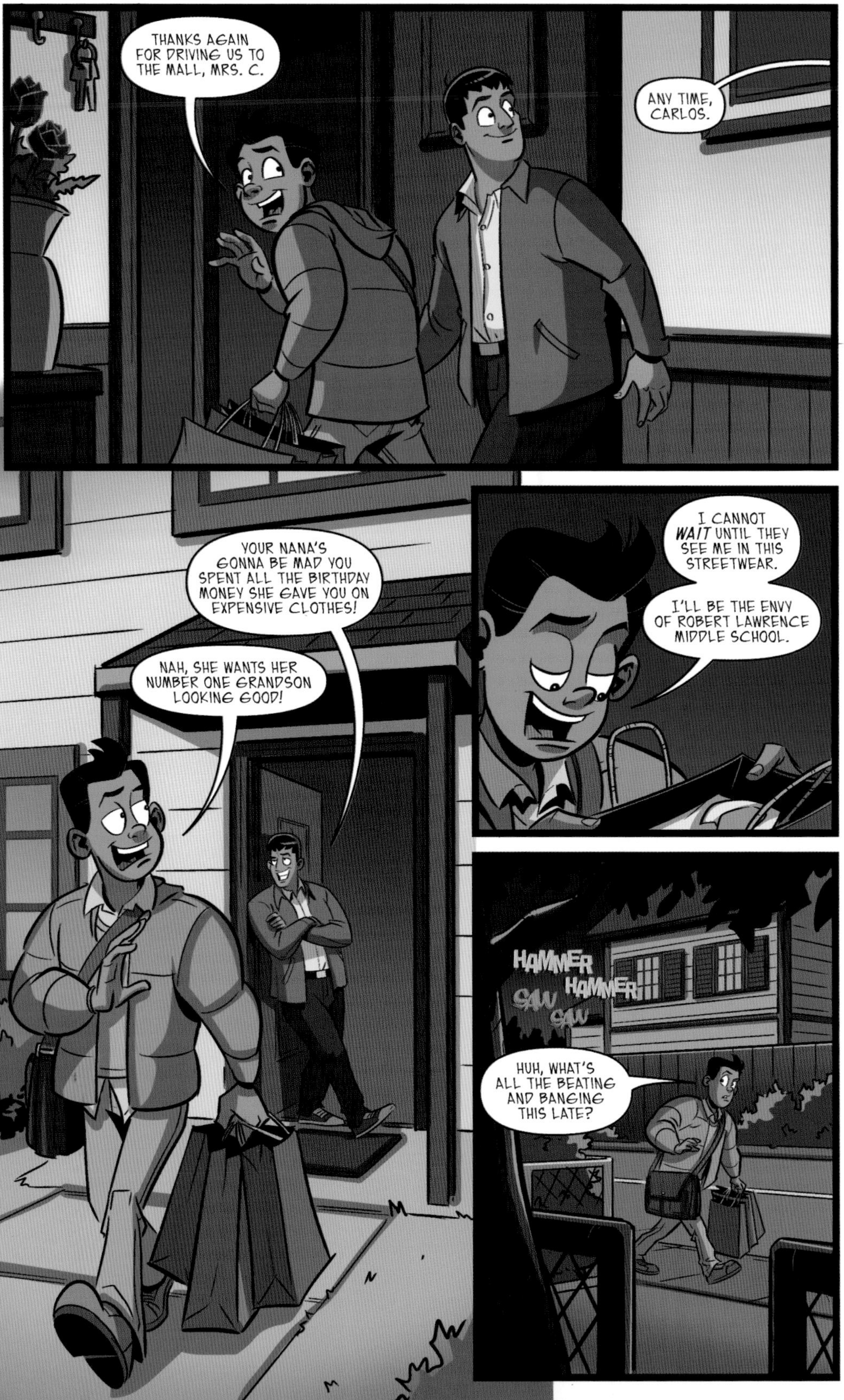
THANKS AGAIN FOR DRIVING US TO THE MALL, MRS. C.
ANY TIME, CARLOS.
YOUR NANA'S GONNA BE MAD YOU SPENT ALL THE BIRTHDAY MONEY SHE GAVE YOU ON EXPENSIVE CLOTHES!
NAH, SHE WANTS HER NUMBER ONE GRANDSON LOOKING GOOD!
I CANNOT *WAIT* UNTIL THEY SEE ME IN THIS STREETWEAR.
I'LL BE THE ENVY OF ROBERT LAWRENCE MIDDLE SCHOOL.
HAMMER
HAMMER!
SAW
SAW
HUH, WHAT'S ALL THE BEATING AND BANGING THIS LATE?

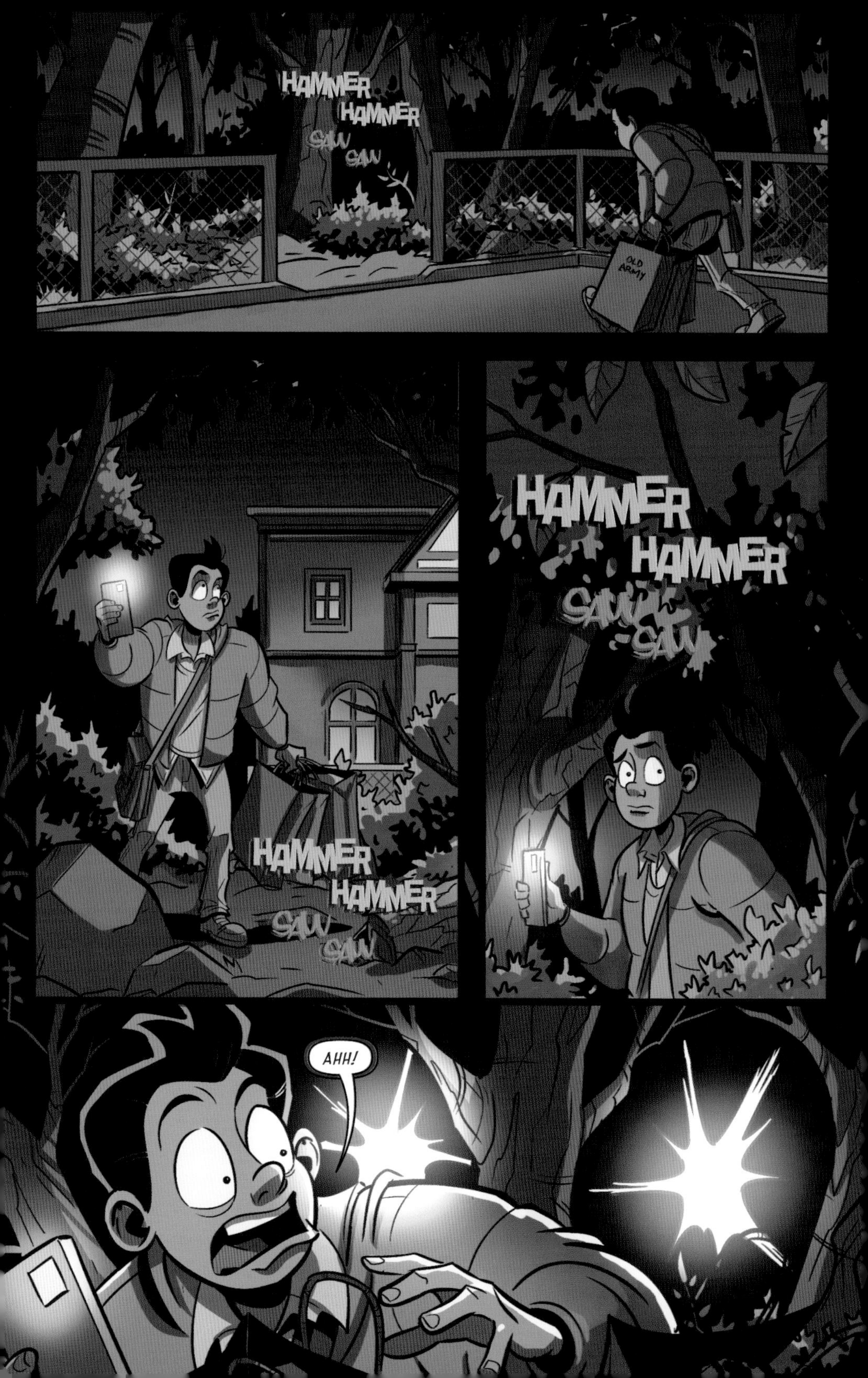
HAMMER
HAMMER
SAW
SAW
OLD ARMY
HAMMER
HAMMER
SAW
SAW
HAMMER
HAMMER
SAW
SAW
AHH!

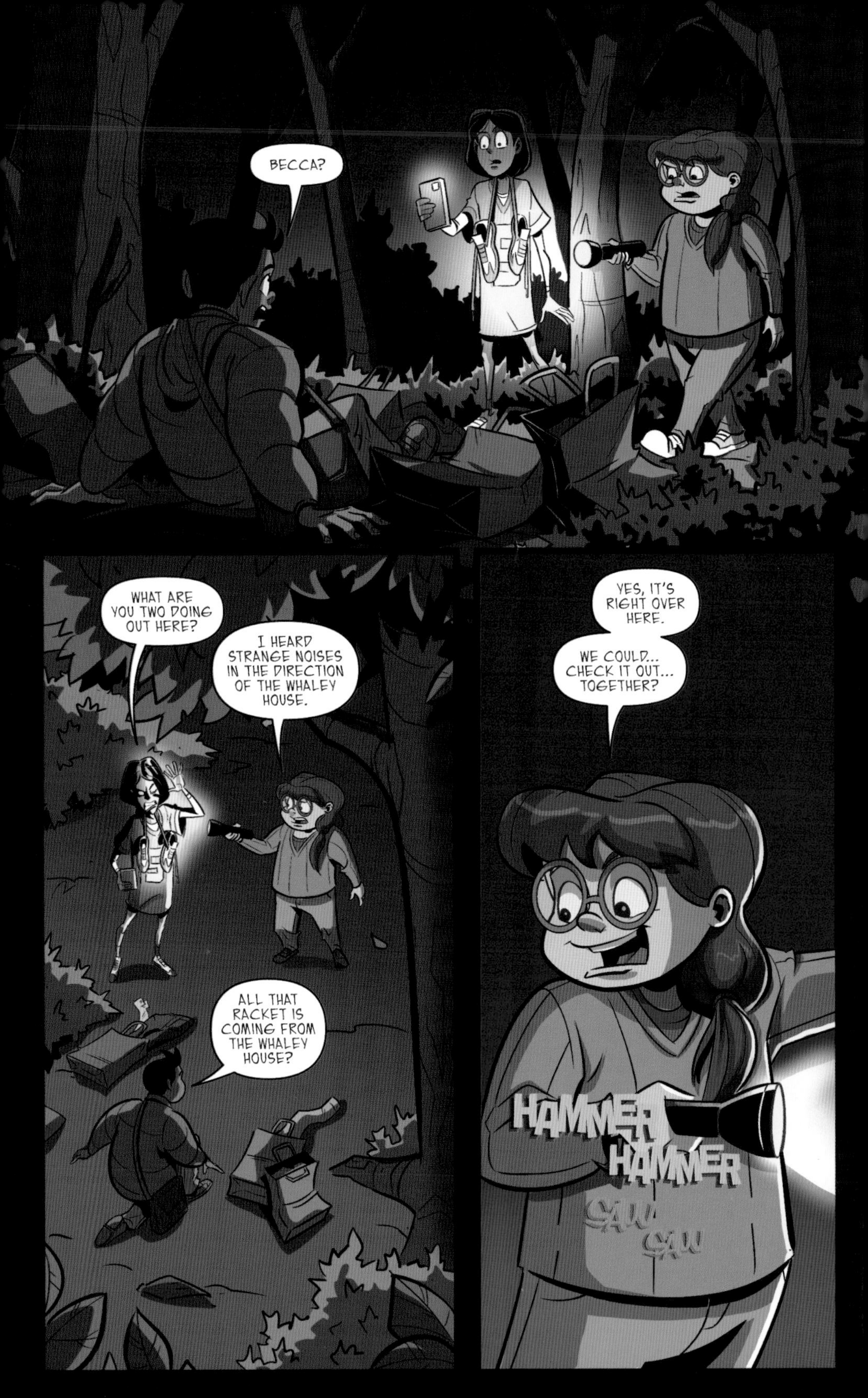

BECCA?
WHAT ARE YOU TWO DOING OUT HERE?
I HEARD STRANGE NOISES IN THE DIRECTION OF THE WHALEY HOUSE.
ALL THAT RACKET IS COMING FROM THE WHALEY HOUSE?
YES, IT'S RIGHT OVER HERE.
WE COULD... CHECK IT OUT... TOGETHER?
HAMMER HAMMER
SAW SAW

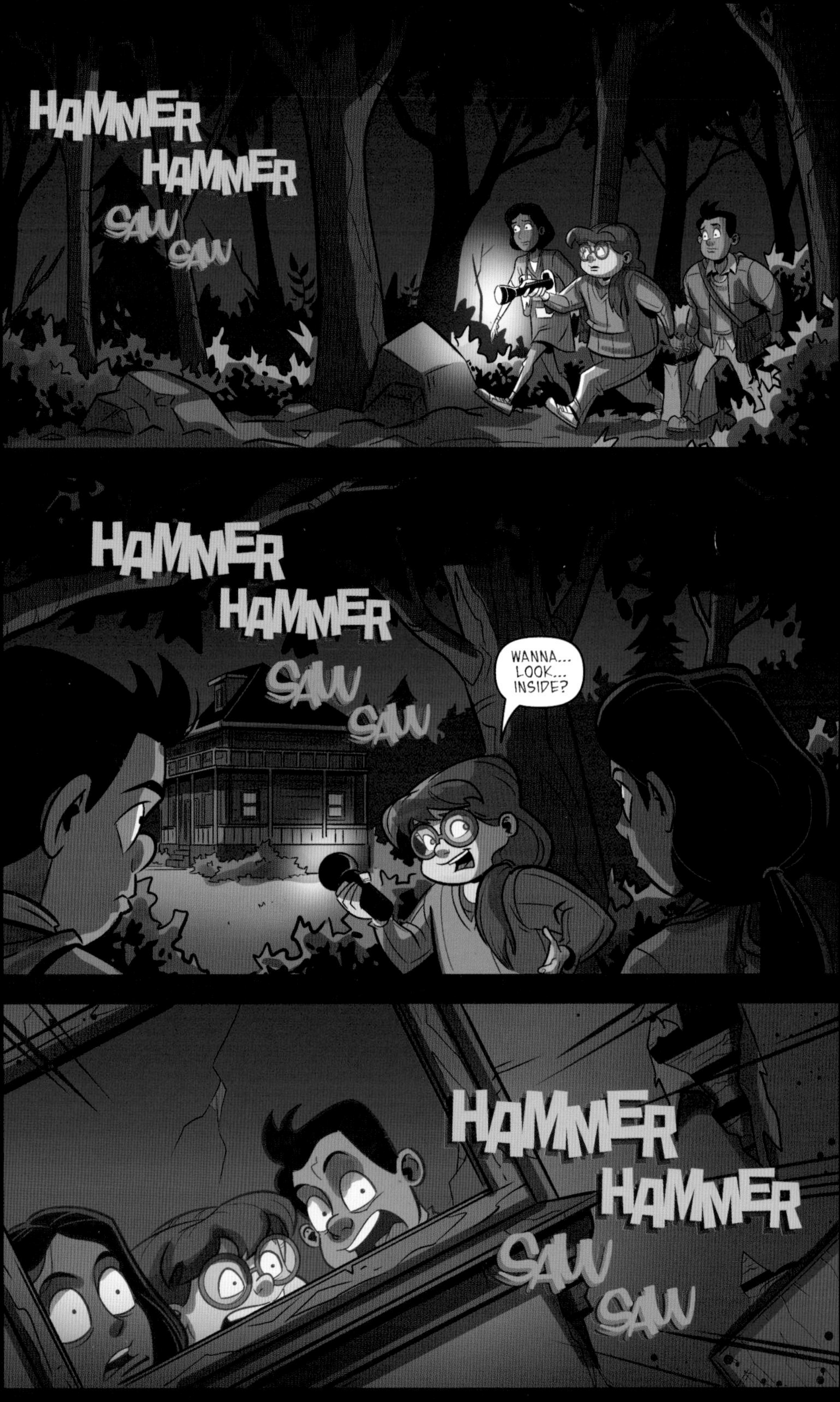
HAMMER
HAMMER
SAW
SAW
HAMMER
HAMMER
SAW
SAW
WANNA... LOOK... INSIDE?
HAMMER
HAMMER
SAW
SAW

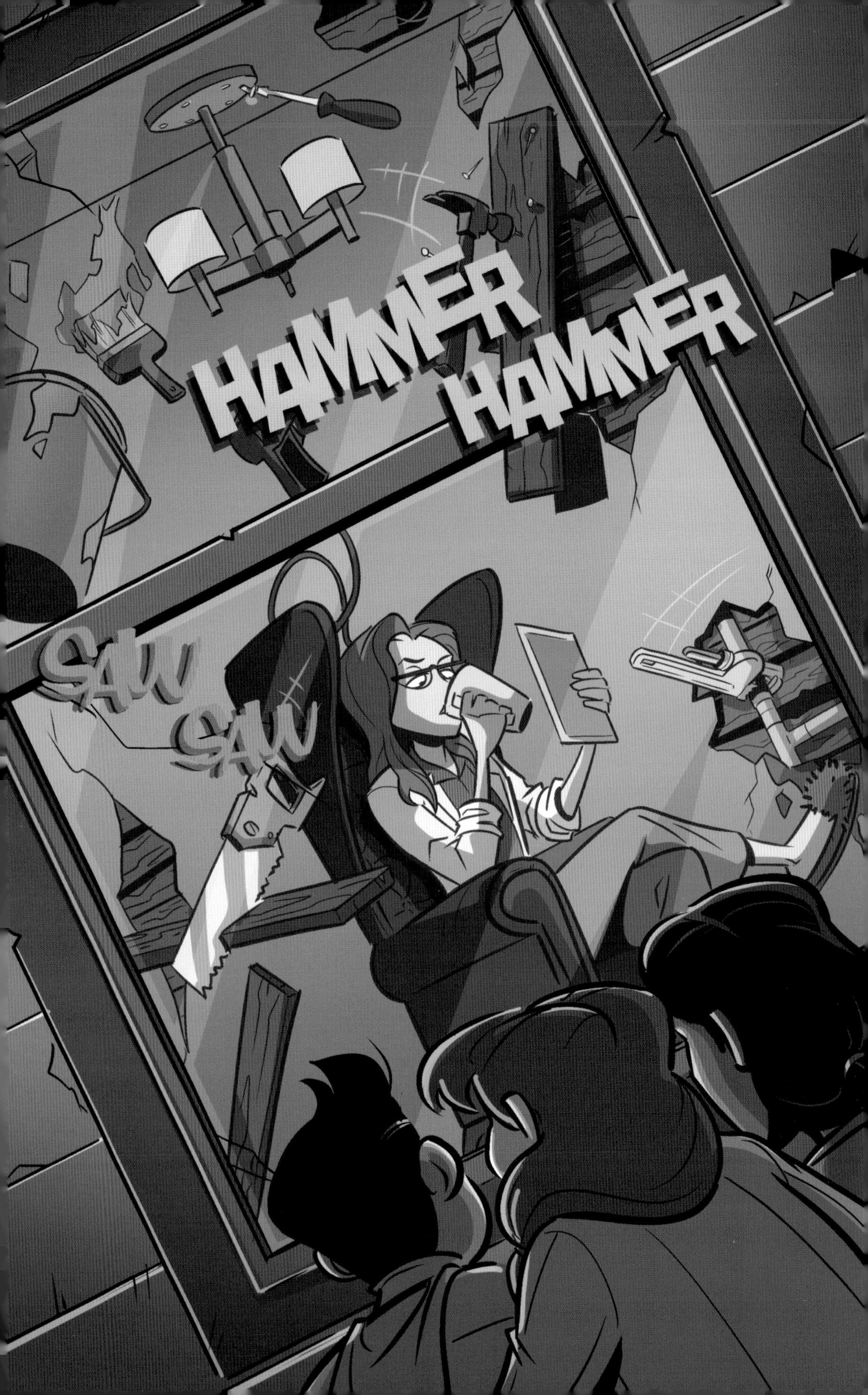
HAMMER
HAMMER
SAW
SAW

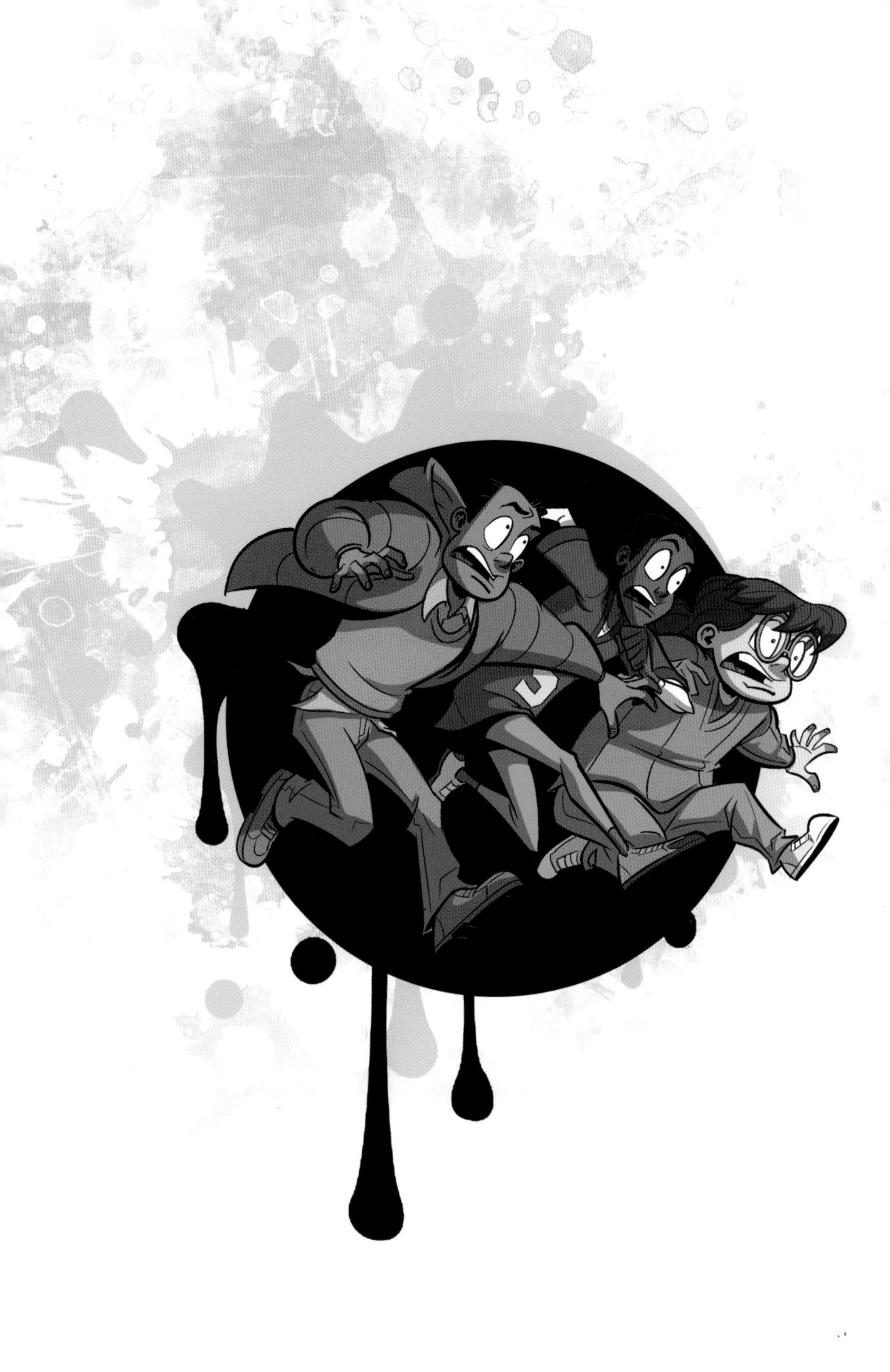

ART BY **CHRIS FENOGLIO**

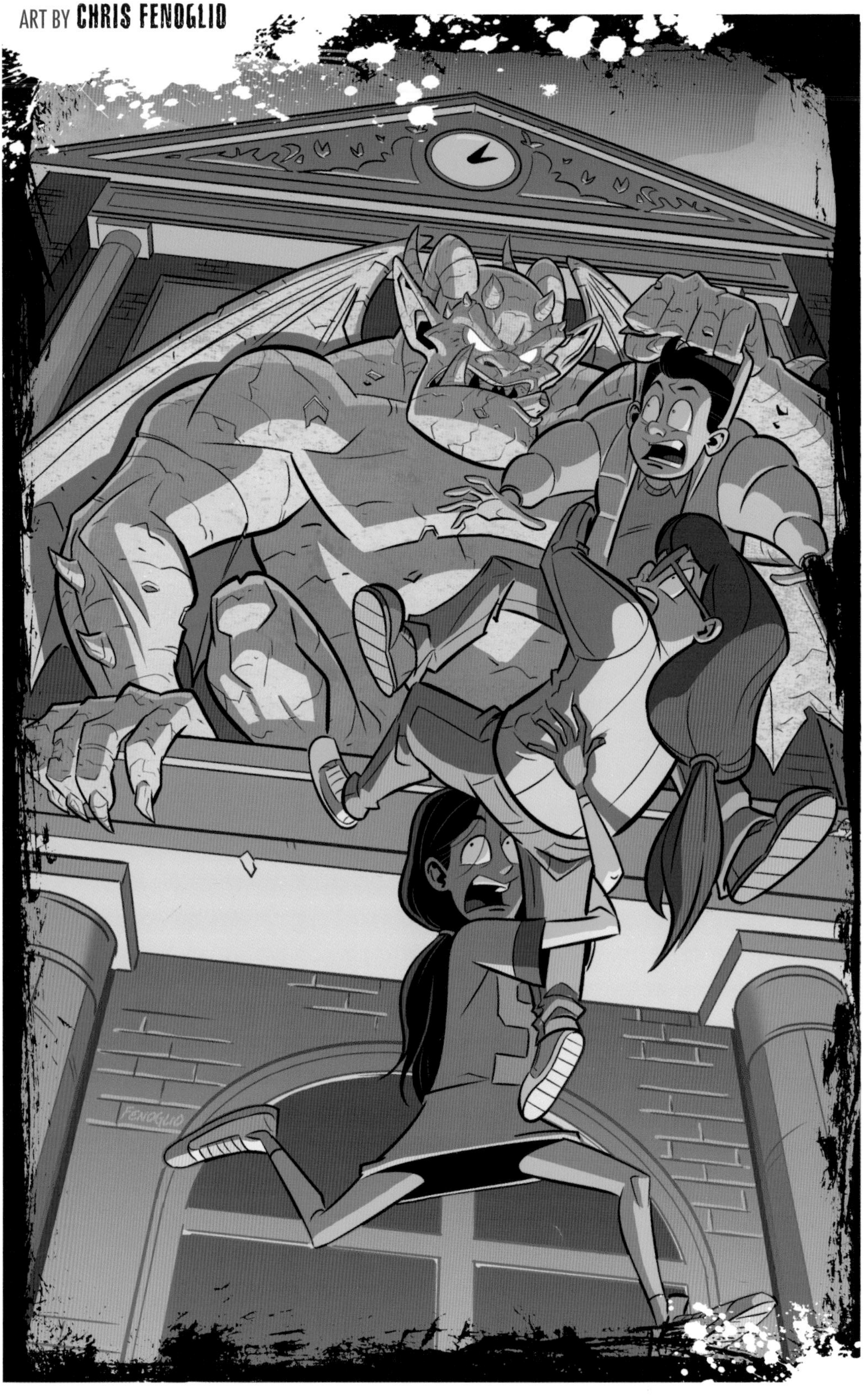
FENOGLIO

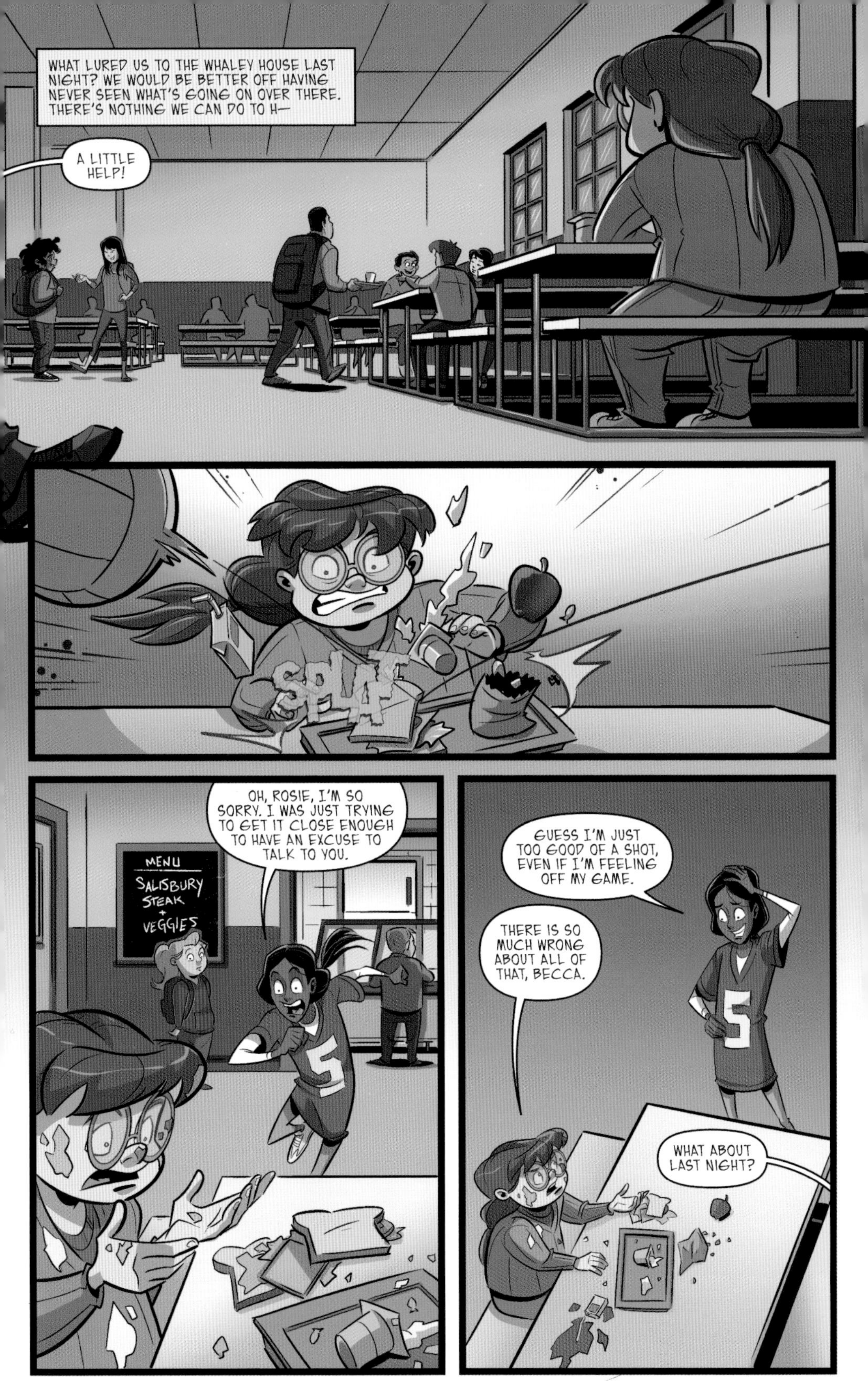
WHAT LURED US TO THE WHALEY HOUSE LAST NIGHT? WE WOULD BE BETTER OFF HAVING NEVER SEEN WHAT'S GOING ON OVER THERE. THERE'S NOTHING WE CAN DO TO H—
A LITTLE HELP!
SPLAT
OH, ROSIE, I'M SO SORRY. I WAS JUST TRYING TO GET IT CLOSE ENOUGH TO HAVE AN EXCUSE TO TALK TO YOU.
MENU
SALISBURY STEAK + VEGGIES
GUESS I'M JUST TOO GOOD OF A SHOT, EVEN IF I'M FEELING OFF MY GAME.
THERE IS SO MUCH WRONG ABOUT ALL OF THAT, BECCA.
WHAT ABOUT LAST NIGHT?

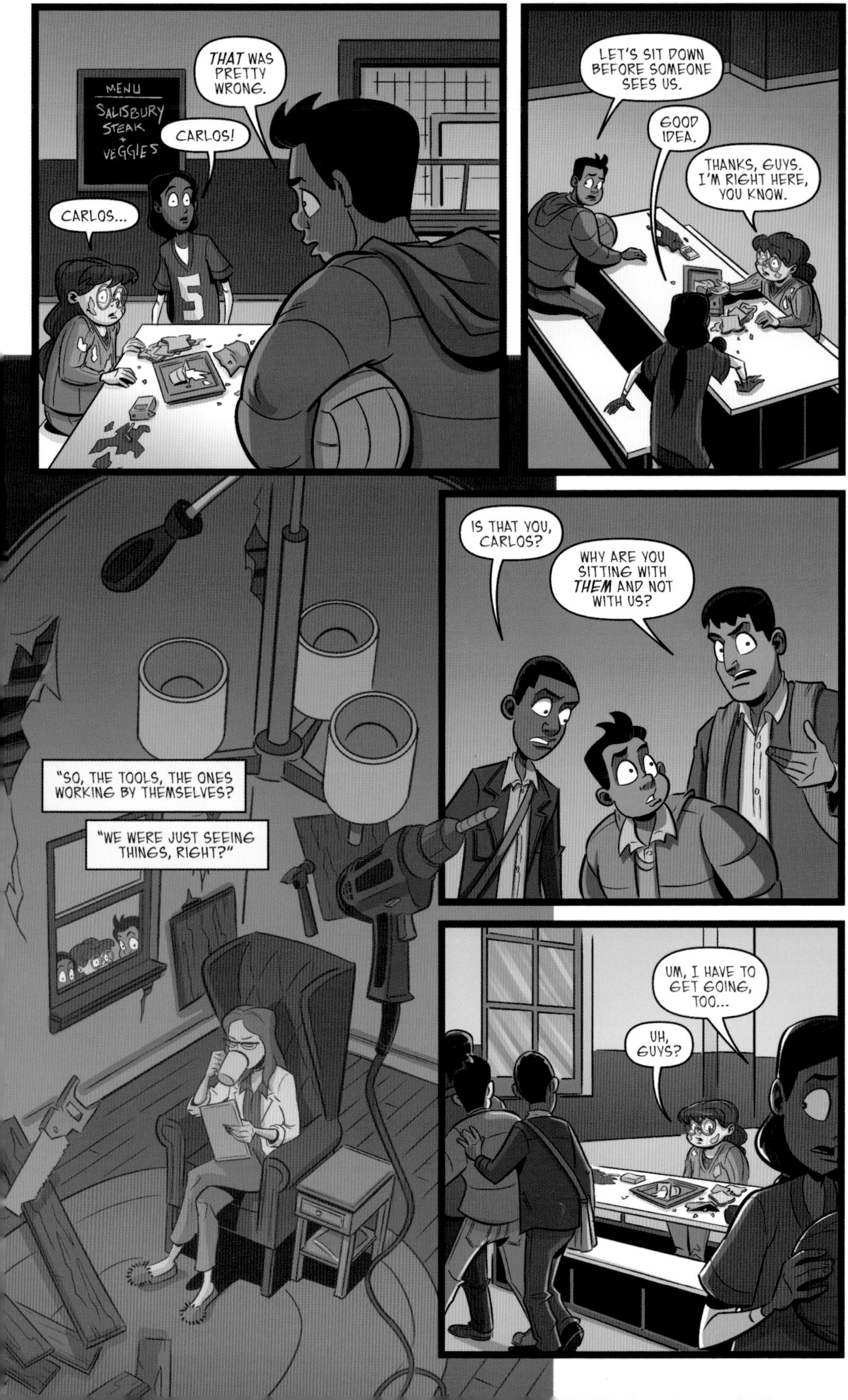
MENU
SALISBURY STEAK + VEGGIES
THAT WAS PRETTY WRONG.
CARLOS!
CARLOS...
LET'S SIT DOWN BEFORE SOMEONE SEES US.
GOOD IDEA.
THANKS, GUYS. I'M RIGHT HERE, YOU KNOW.
"SO, THE TOOLS, THE ONES WORKING BY THEMSELVES?
"WE WERE JUST SEEING THINGS, RIGHT?"
IS THAT YOU, CARLOS?
WHY ARE YOU SITTING WITH THEM AND NOT WITH US?
UM, I HAVE TO GET GOING, TOO...
UH, GUYS?

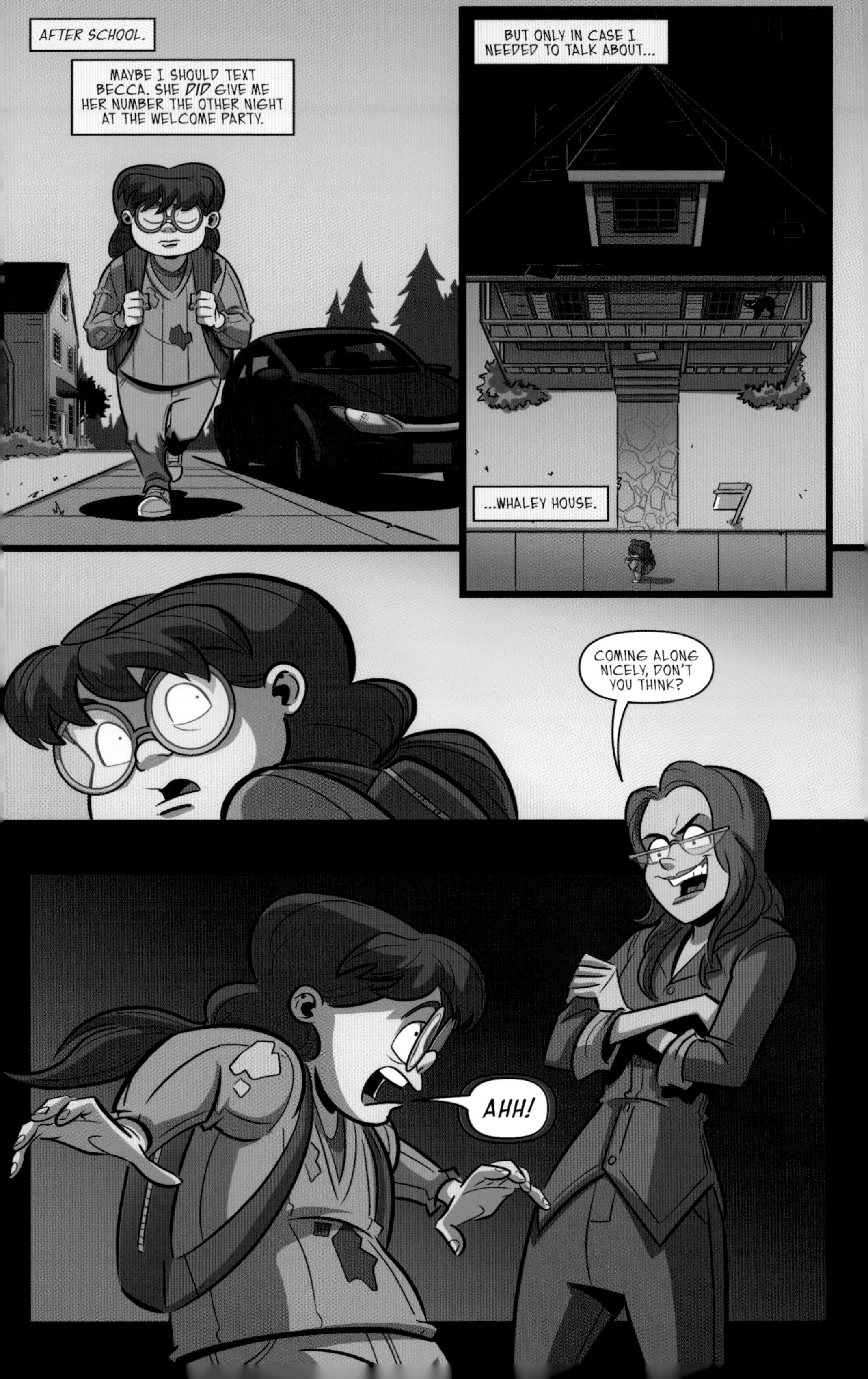
AFTER SCHOOL.
MAYBE I SHOULD TEXT BECCA. SHE *DID* GIVE ME HER NUMBER THE OTHER NIGHT AT THE WELCOME PARTY.
BUT ONLY IN CASE I NEEDED TO TALK ABOUT...
...WHALEY HOUSE.
COMING ALONG NICELY, DON'T YOU THINK?
AHH!

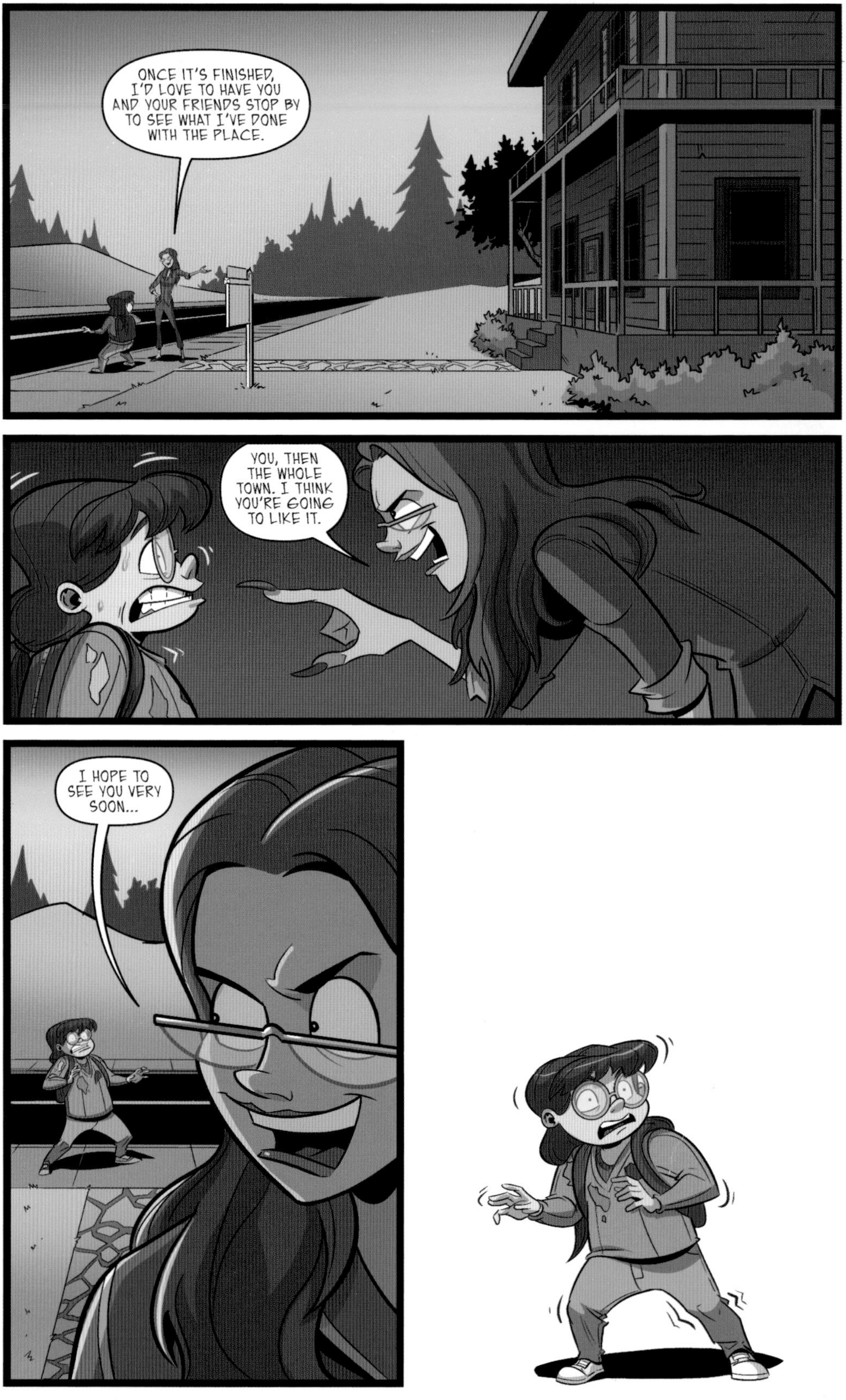
ONCE IT'S FINISHED, I'D LOVE TO HAVE YOU AND YOUR FRIENDS STOP BY TO SEE WHAT I'VE DONE WITH THE PLACE.
YOU, THEN THE WHOLE TOWN. I THINK YOU'RE GOING TO LIKE IT.
I HOPE TO SEE YOU VERY SOON...

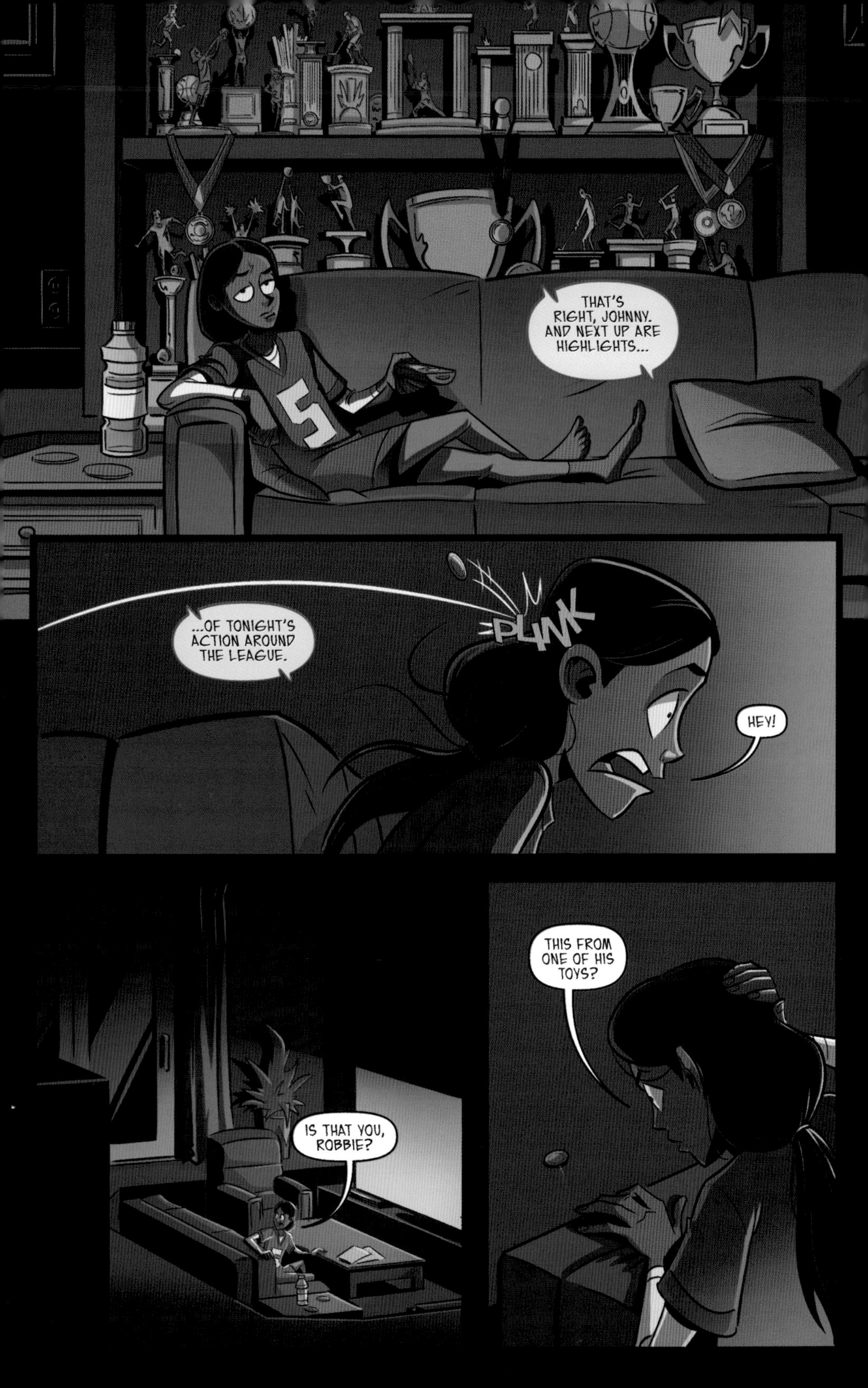
THAT'S RIGHT, JOHNNY. AND NEXT UP ARE HIGHLIGHTS...
...OF TONIGHT'S ACTION AROUND THE LEAGUE.
PLINK
HEY!
IS THAT YOU, ROBBIE?
THIS FROM ONE OF HIS TOYS?

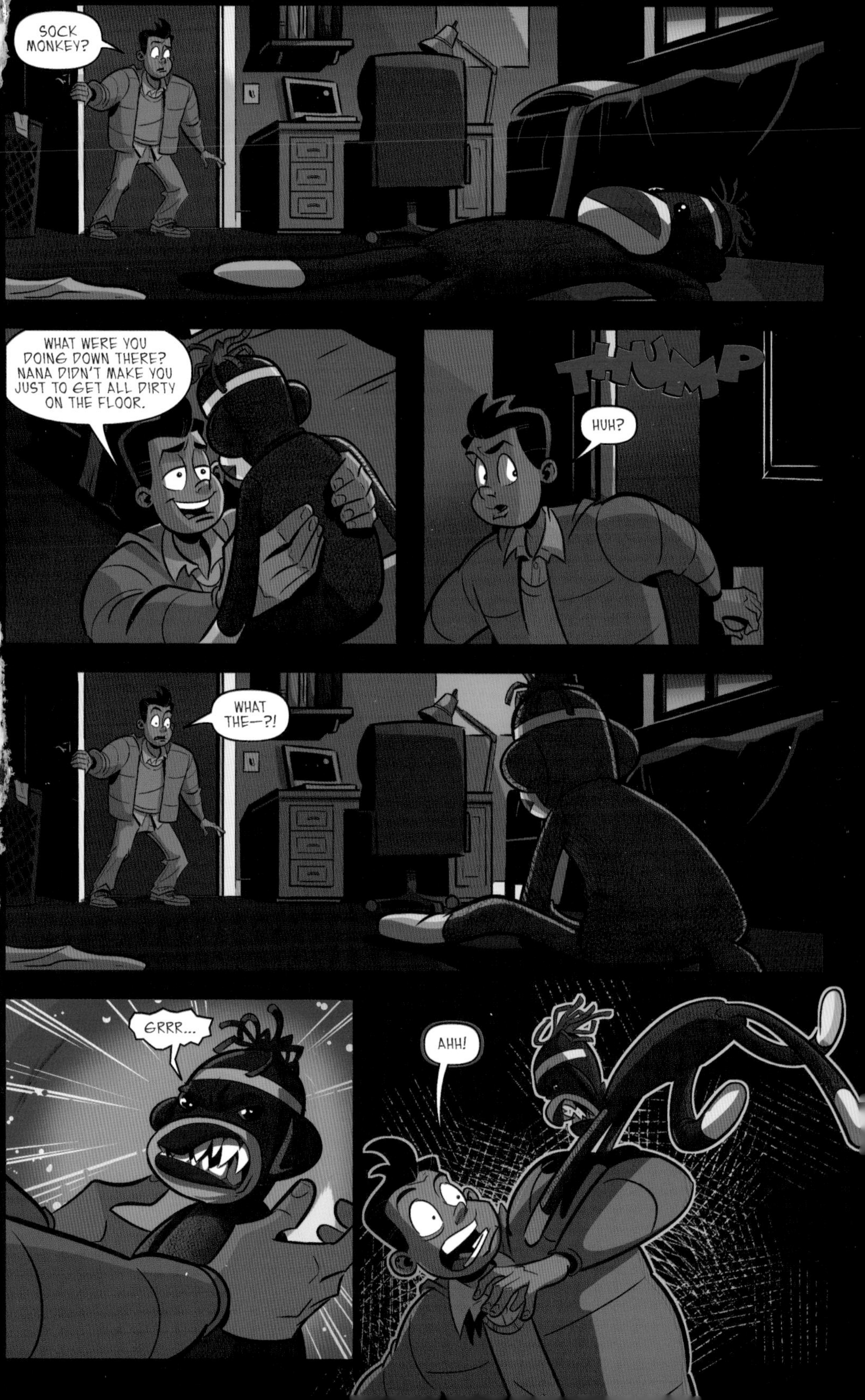
SOCK MONKEY?
WHAT WERE YOU DOING DOWN THERE? NANA DIDN'T MAKE YOU JUST TO GET ALL DIRTY ON THE FLOOR.
THUMP
HUH?
WHAT THE—?!
GRRR...
AHH!

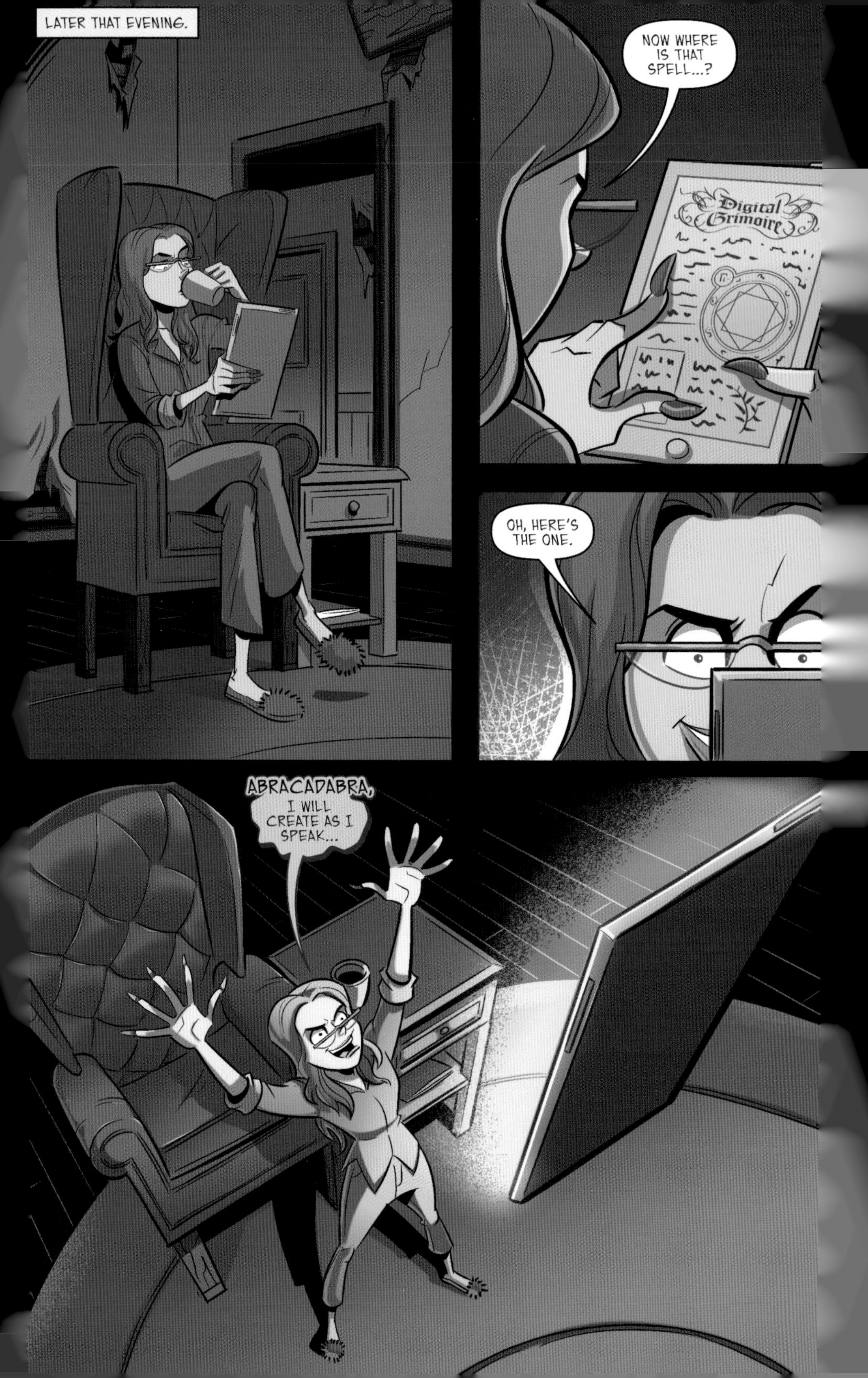
LATER THAT EVENING.
NOW WHERE IS THAT SPELL...?
Digital Grimoire
OH, HERE'S THE ONE.
ABRACADABRA, I WILL CREATE AS I SPEAK...

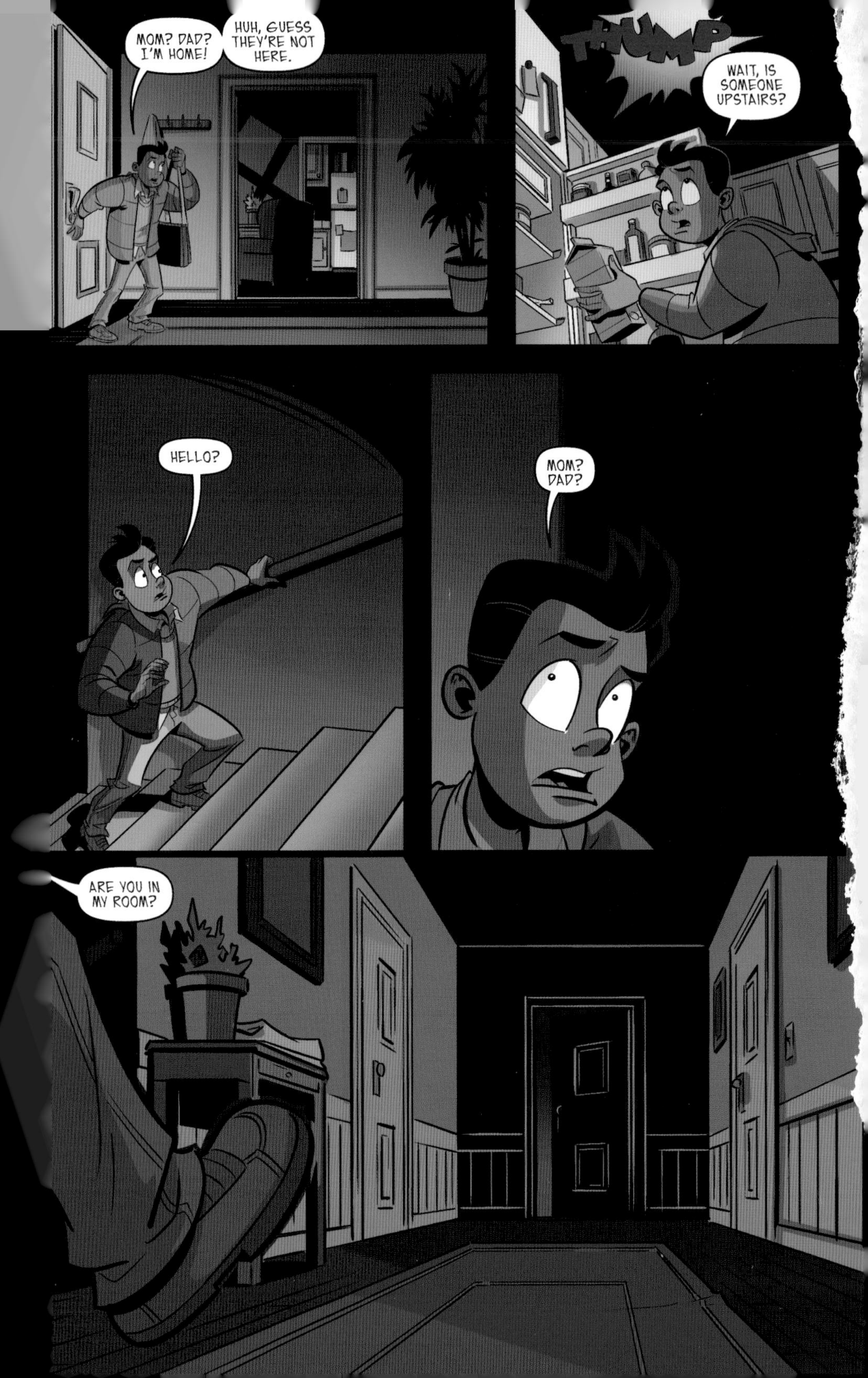
MOM? DAD? I'M HOME!
HUH, GUESS THEY'RE NOT HERE.
THUMP
WAIT, IS SOMEONE UPSTAIRS?
HELLO?
MOM? DAD?
ARE YOU IN MY ROOM?

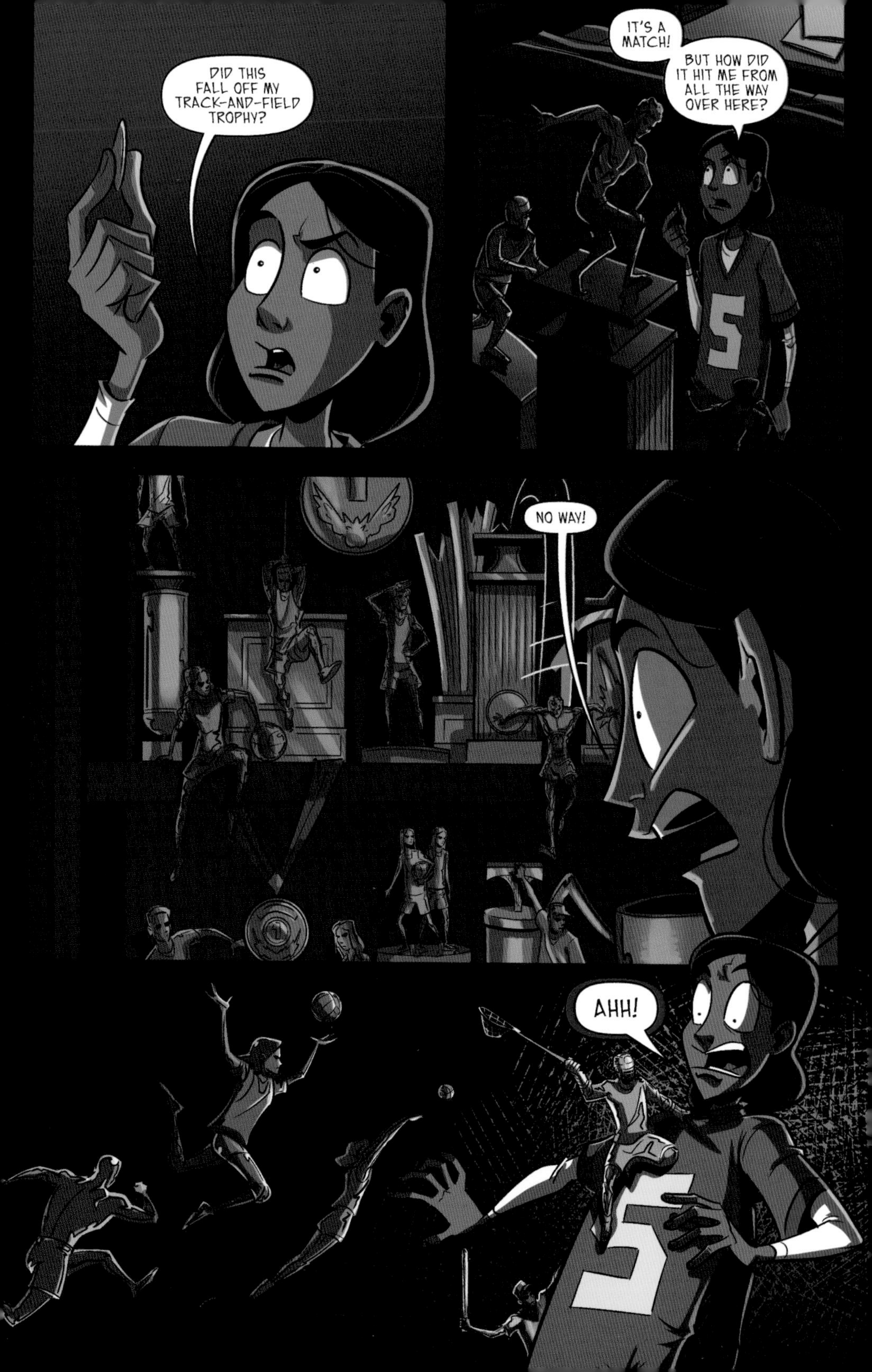
DID THIS FALL OFF MY TRACK-AND-FIELD TROPHY?
IT'S A MATCH!
BUT HOW DID IT HIT ME FROM ALL THE WAY OVER HERE?
NO WAY!
AHH!

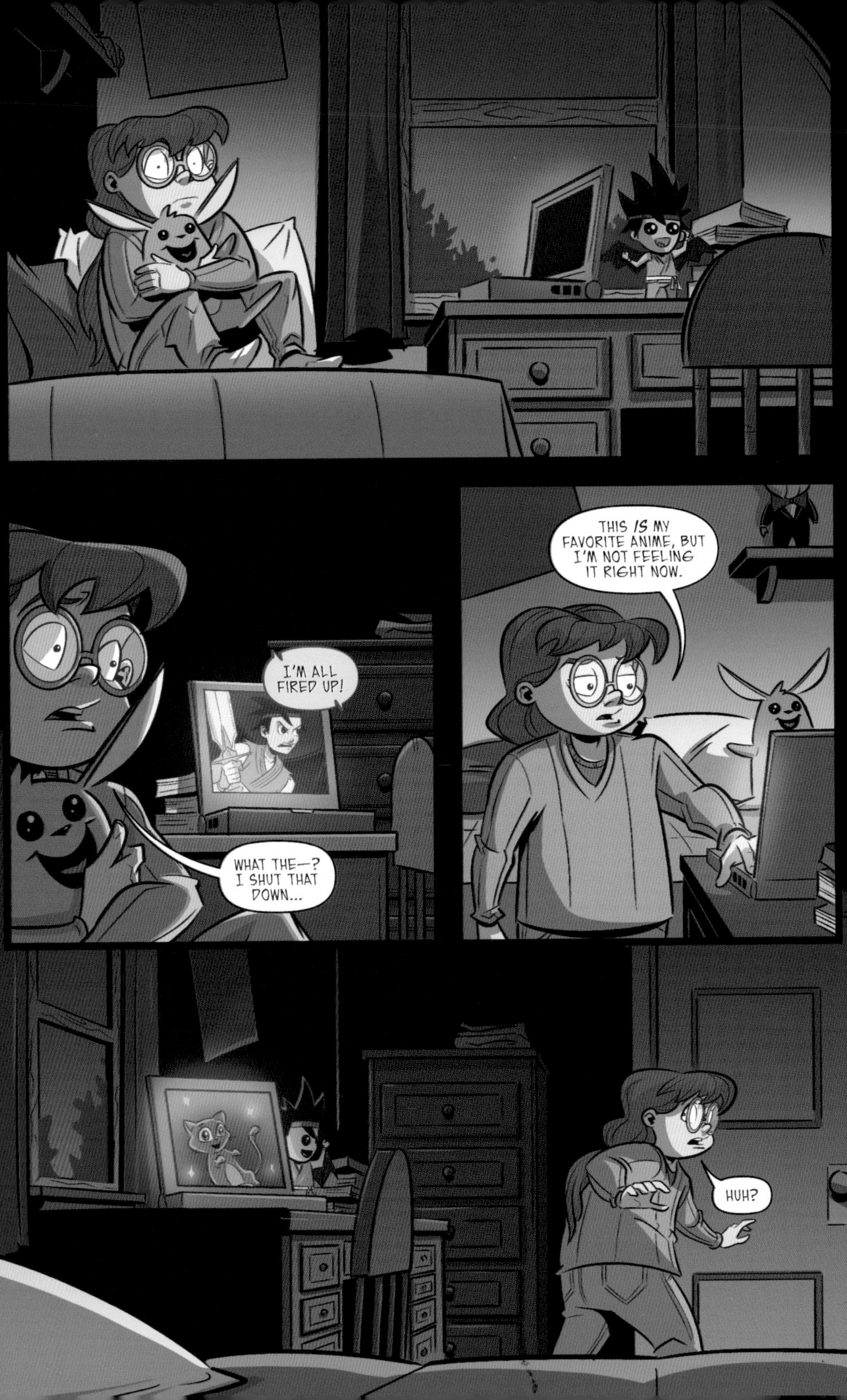
I'M ALL FIRED UP!
WHAT THE—? I SHUT THAT DOWN...
THIS IS MY FAVORITE ANIME, BUT I'M NOT FEELING IT RIGHT NOW.
HUH?

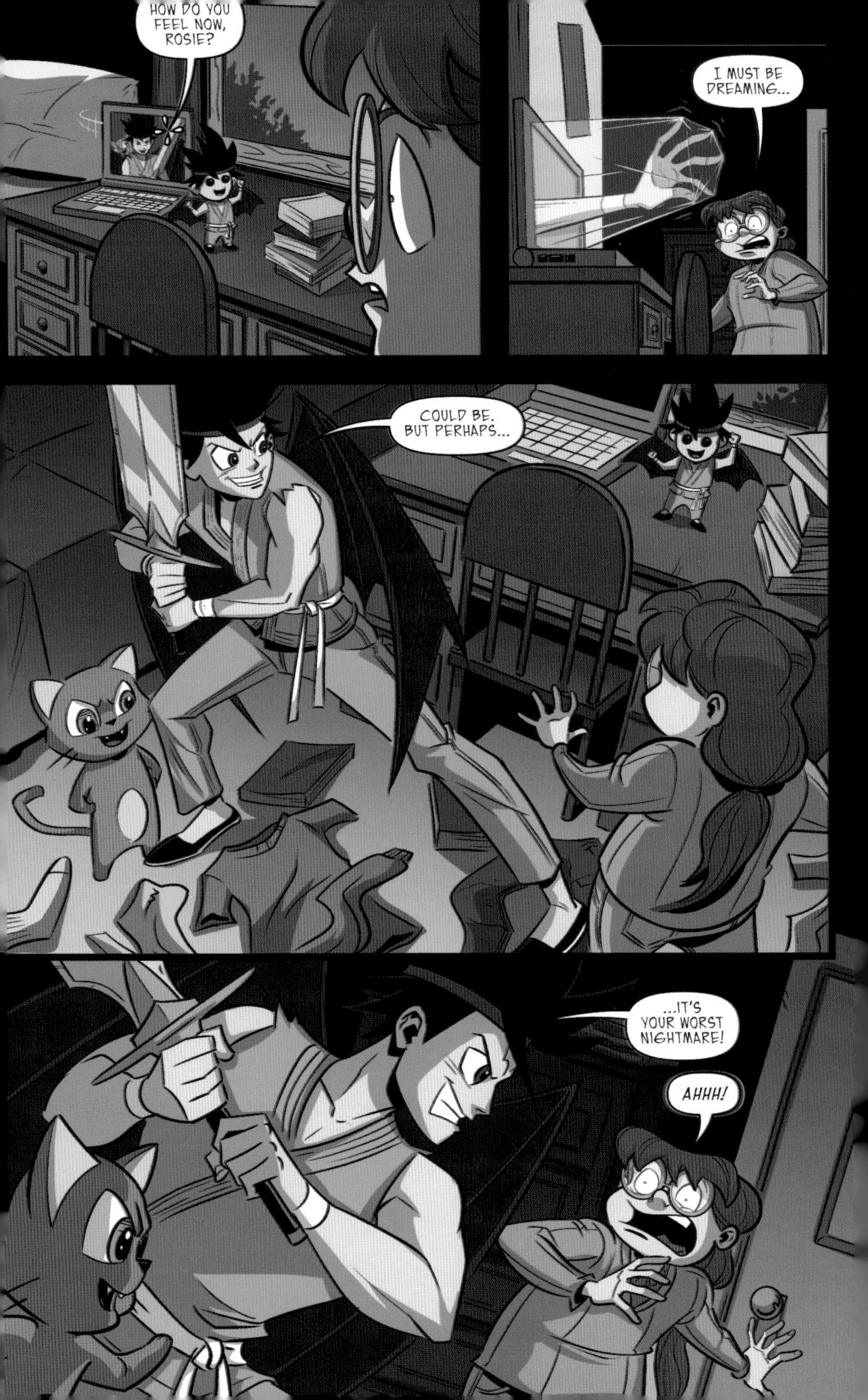
HOW DO YOU FEEL NOW, ROSIE?
I MUST BE DREAMING...
COULD BE. BUT PERHAPS...
...IT'S YOUR WORST NIGHTMARE!
AHHH!

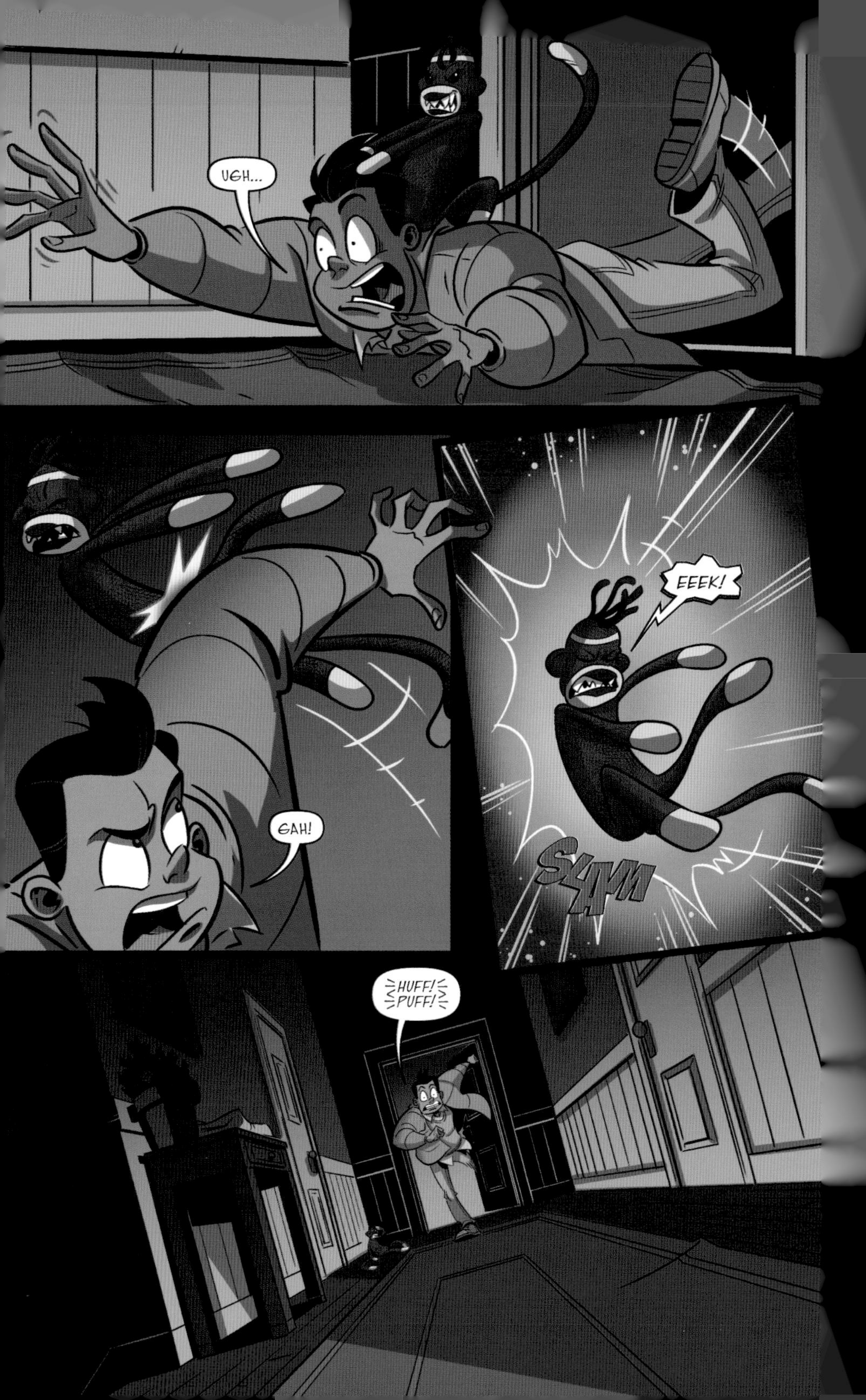
UGH...
GAH!
EEEK!
SLAM
HUFF!
PUFF!

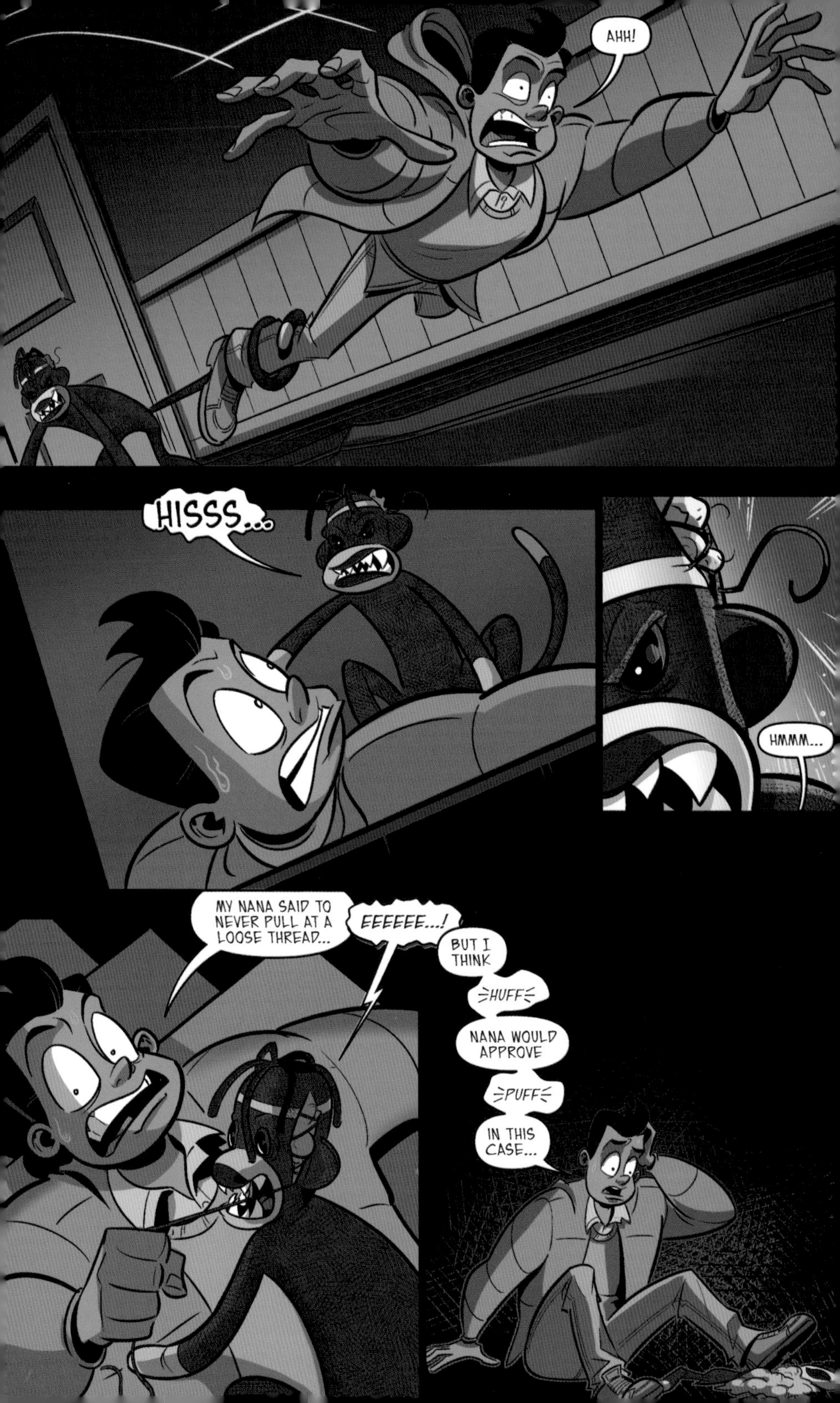
AHH!
HISSS...
HMMM...
MY NANA SAID TO NEVER PULL AT A LOOSE THREAD...
EEEEEE...!
BUT I THINK
HUFF
NANA WOULD APPROVE
PUFF
IN THIS CASE...

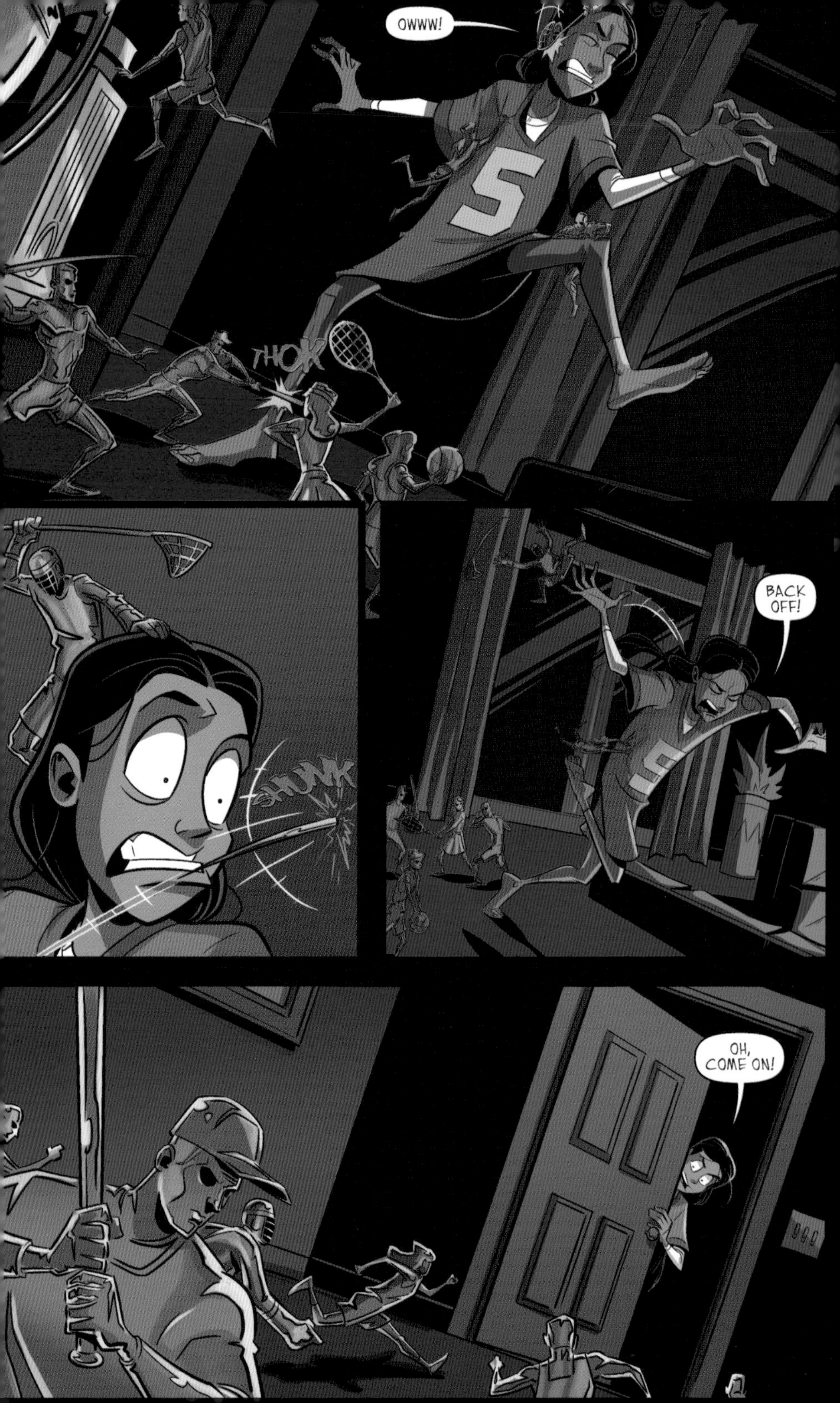
OWWW!
THOK
SHUNK
BACK OFF!
OH, COME ON!

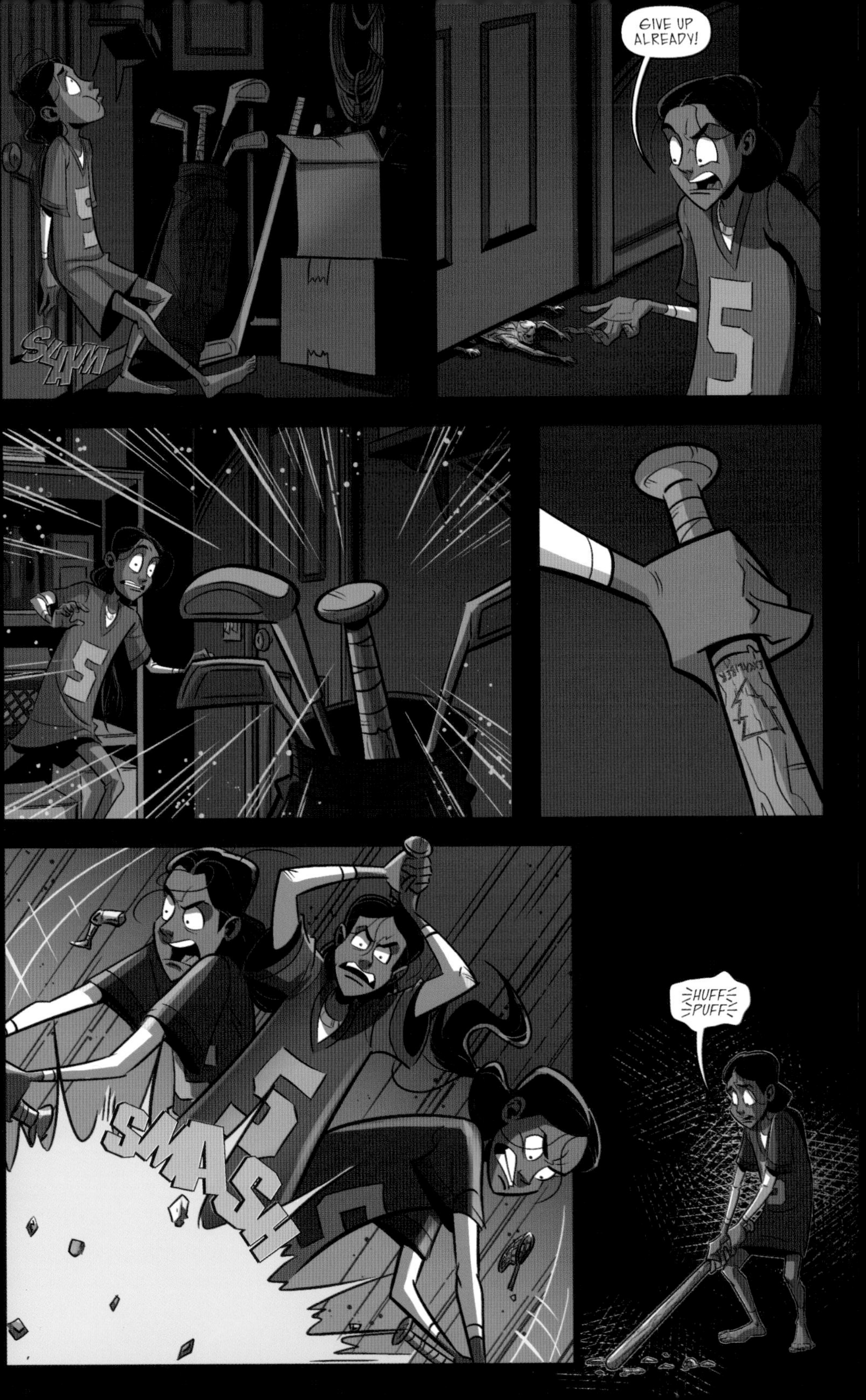
SLAM
GIVE UP ALREADY!
SMASH
HUFF PUFF

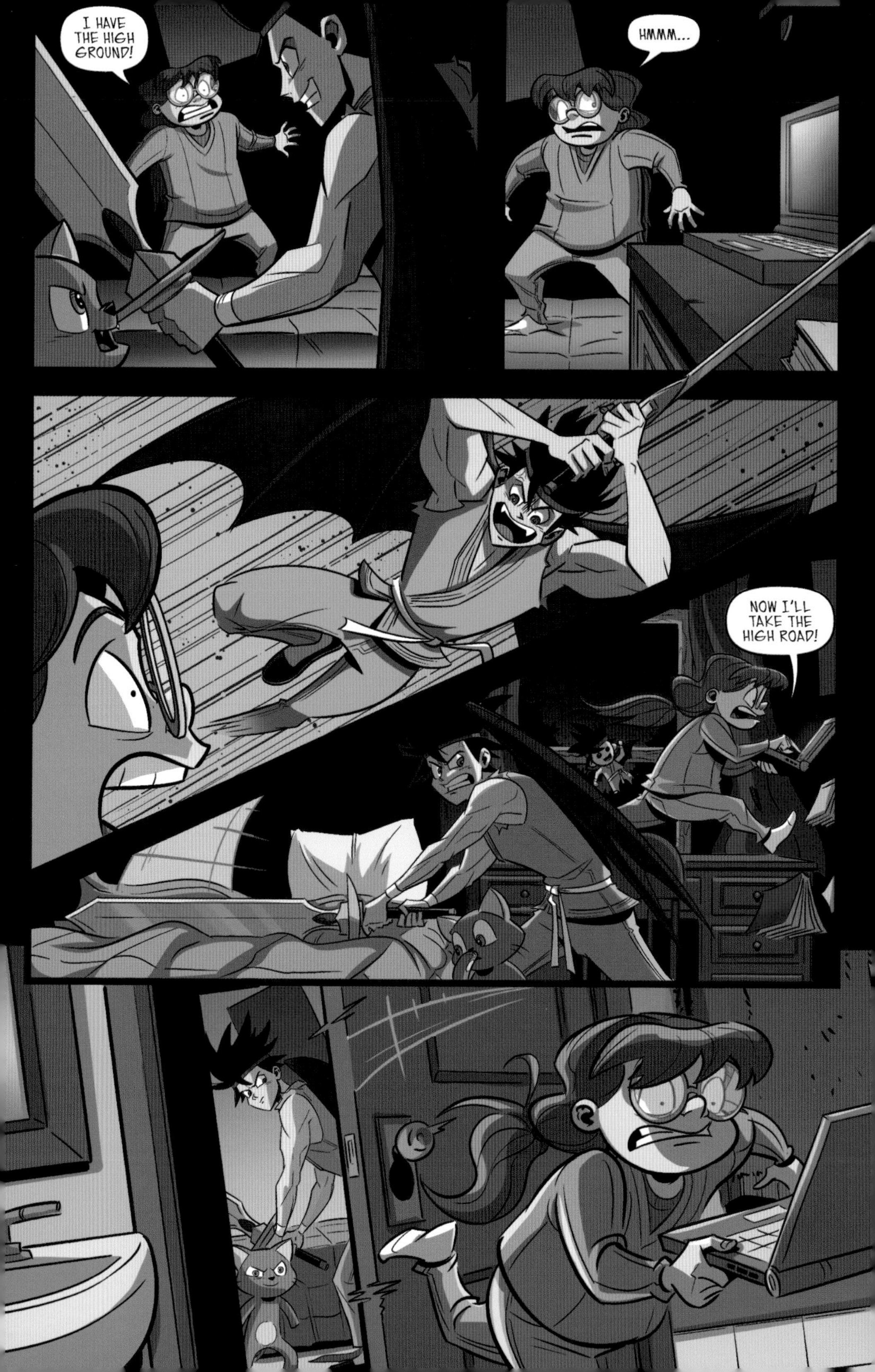
I HAVE THE HIGH GROUND!
HMMM...
NOW I'LL TAKE THE HIGH ROAD!

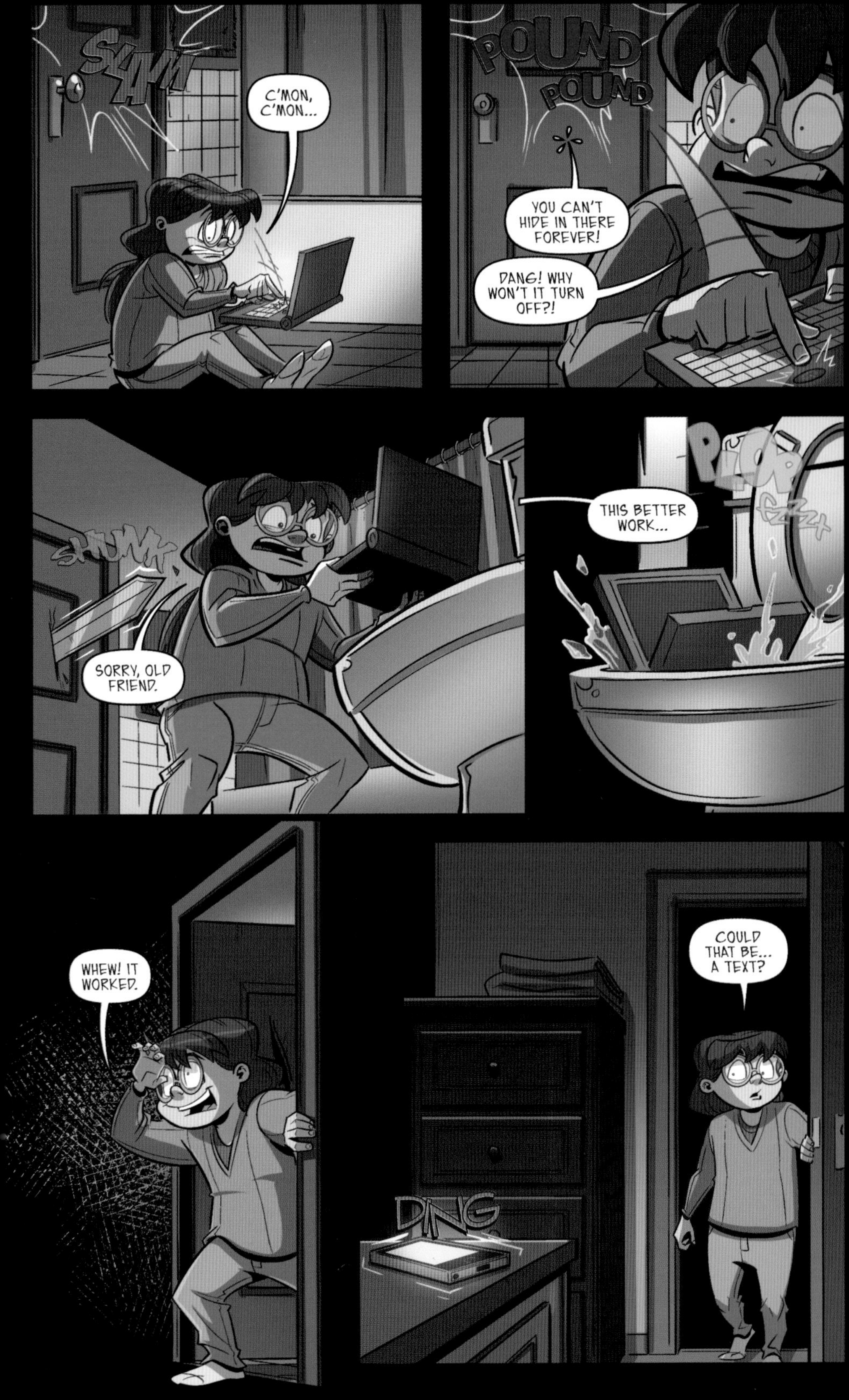
SLAM
C'MON, C'MON...
POUND POUND
YOU CAN'T HIDE IN THERE FOREVER!
DANG! WHY WON'T IT TURN OFF?!
SHUNK
SORRY, OLD FRIEND.
THIS BETTER WORK...
PLOP
FZZZT
WHEW! IT WORKED.
DING
COULD THAT BE... A TEXT?

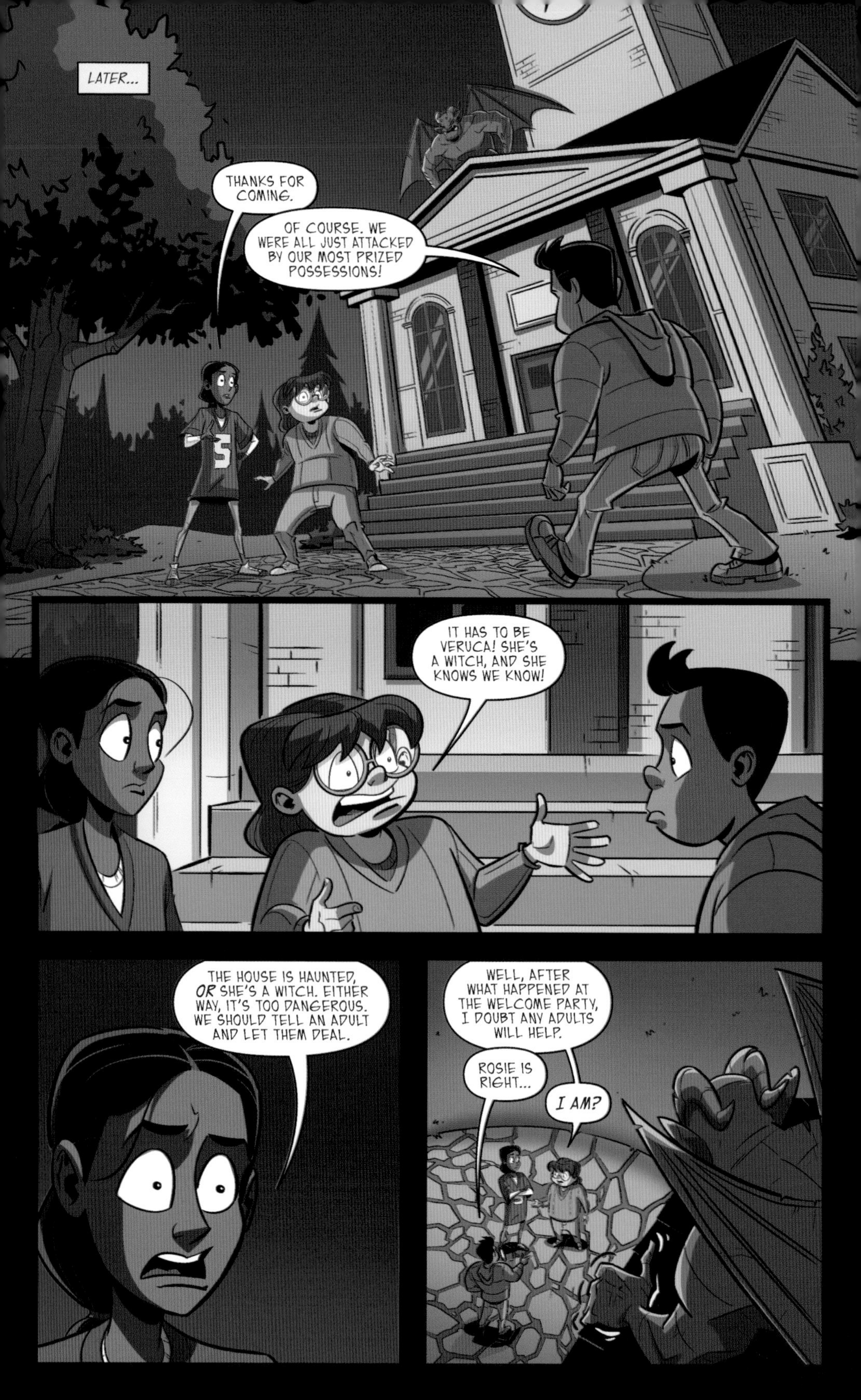
LATER...
THANKS FOR COMING.
OF COURSE. WE WERE ALL JUST ATTACKED BY OUR MOST PRIZED POSSESSIONS!
IT HAS TO BE VERUCA! SHE'S A WITCH, AND SHE KNOWS WE KNOW!
THE HOUSE IS HAUNTED, *OR* SHE'S A WITCH. EITHER WAY, IT'S TOO DANGEROUS. WE SHOULD TELL AN ADULT AND LET THEM DEAL.
WELL, AFTER WHAT HAPPENED AT THE WELCOME PARTY, I DOUBT ANY ADULTS WILL HELP.
ROSIE IS RIGHT...
I AM?

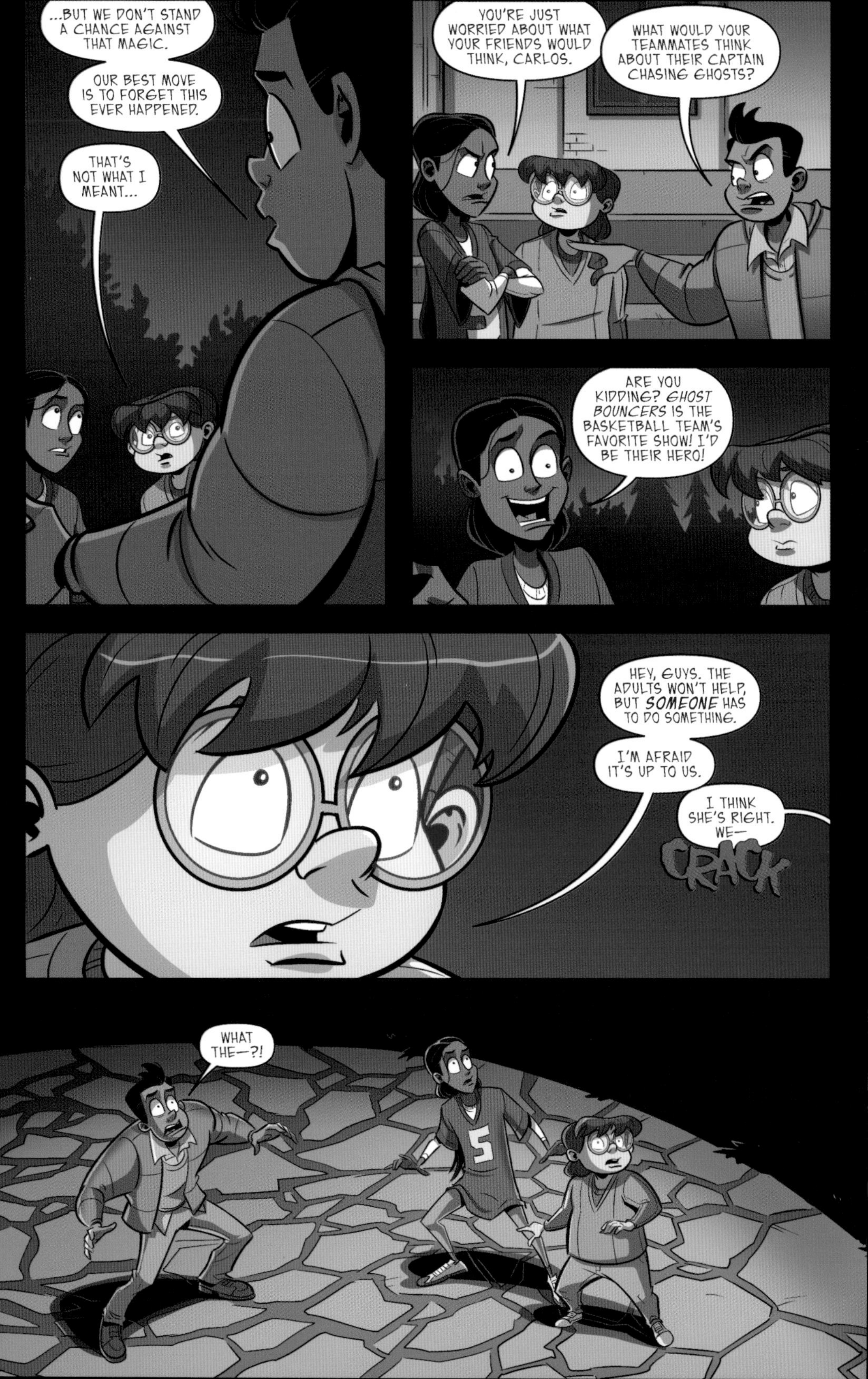
...BUT WE DON'T STAND A CHANCE AGAINST THAT MAGIC.
OUR BEST MOVE IS TO FORGET THIS EVER HAPPENED.
THAT'S NOT WHAT I MEANT...
YOU'RE JUST WORRIED ABOUT WHAT YOUR FRIENDS WOULD THINK, CARLOS.
WHAT WOULD YOUR TEAMMATES THINK ABOUT THEIR CAPTAIN CHASING GHOSTS?
ARE YOU KIDDING? GHOST BOUNCERS IS THE BASKETBALL TEAM'S FAVORITE SHOW! I'D BE THEIR HERO!
HEY, GUYS. THE ADULTS WON'T HELP, BUT SOMEONE HAS TO DO SOMETHING.
I'M AFRAID IT'S UP TO US.
I THINK SHE'S RIGHT. WE—
CRACK
WHAT THE—?!
5

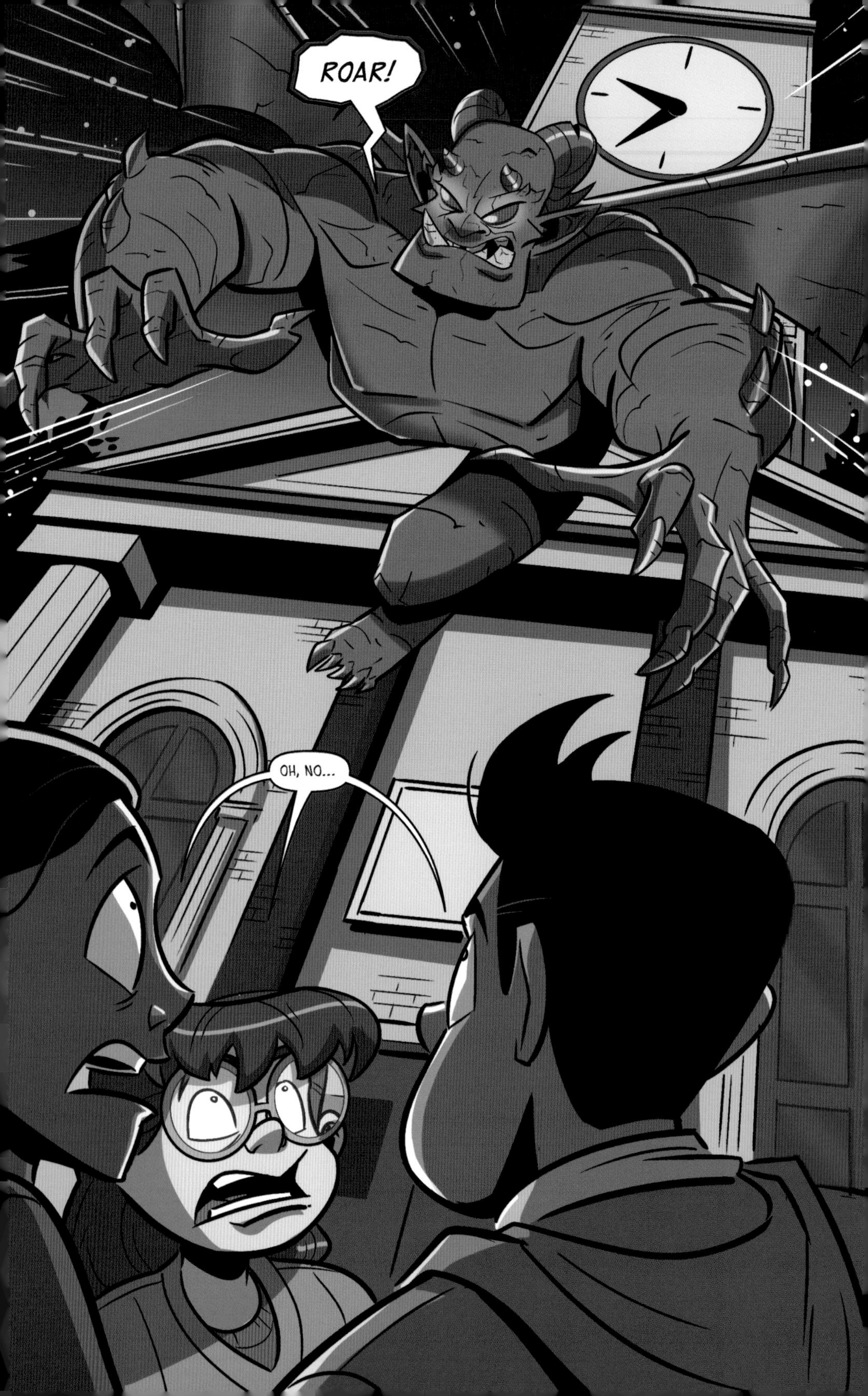
ROAR!
OH, NO...

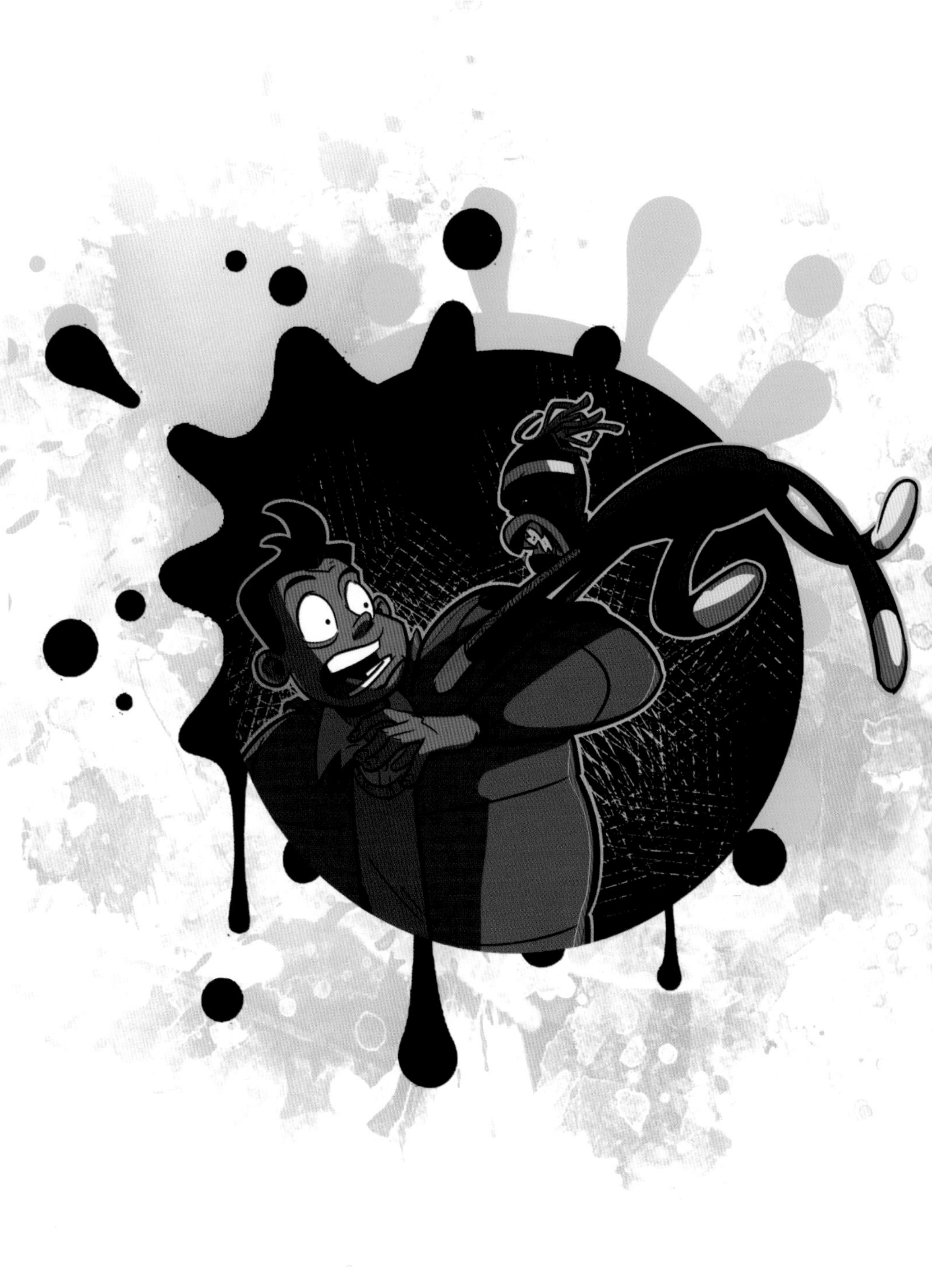

ART BY **CHRIS FENOGLIO**

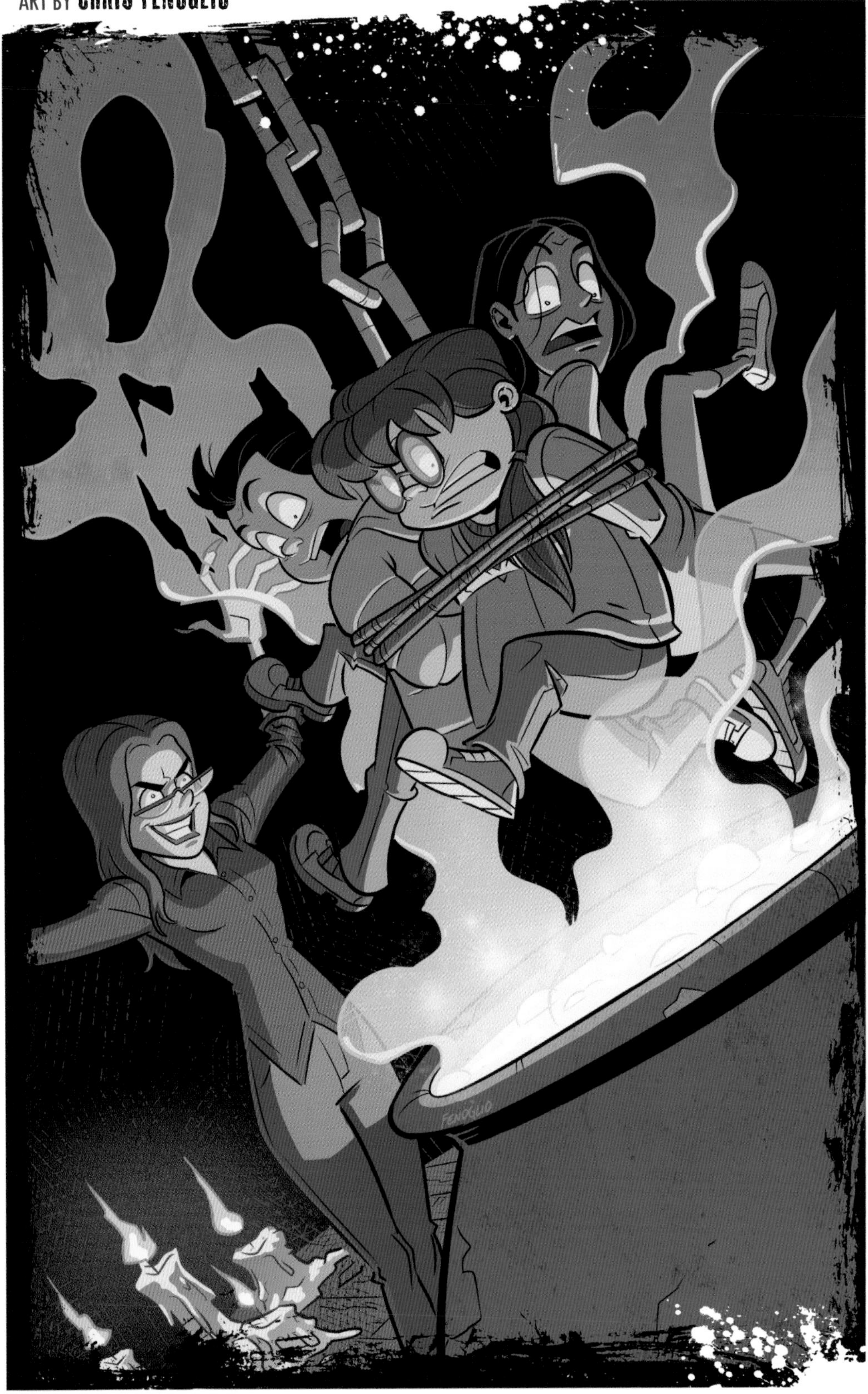
FENOGLIO

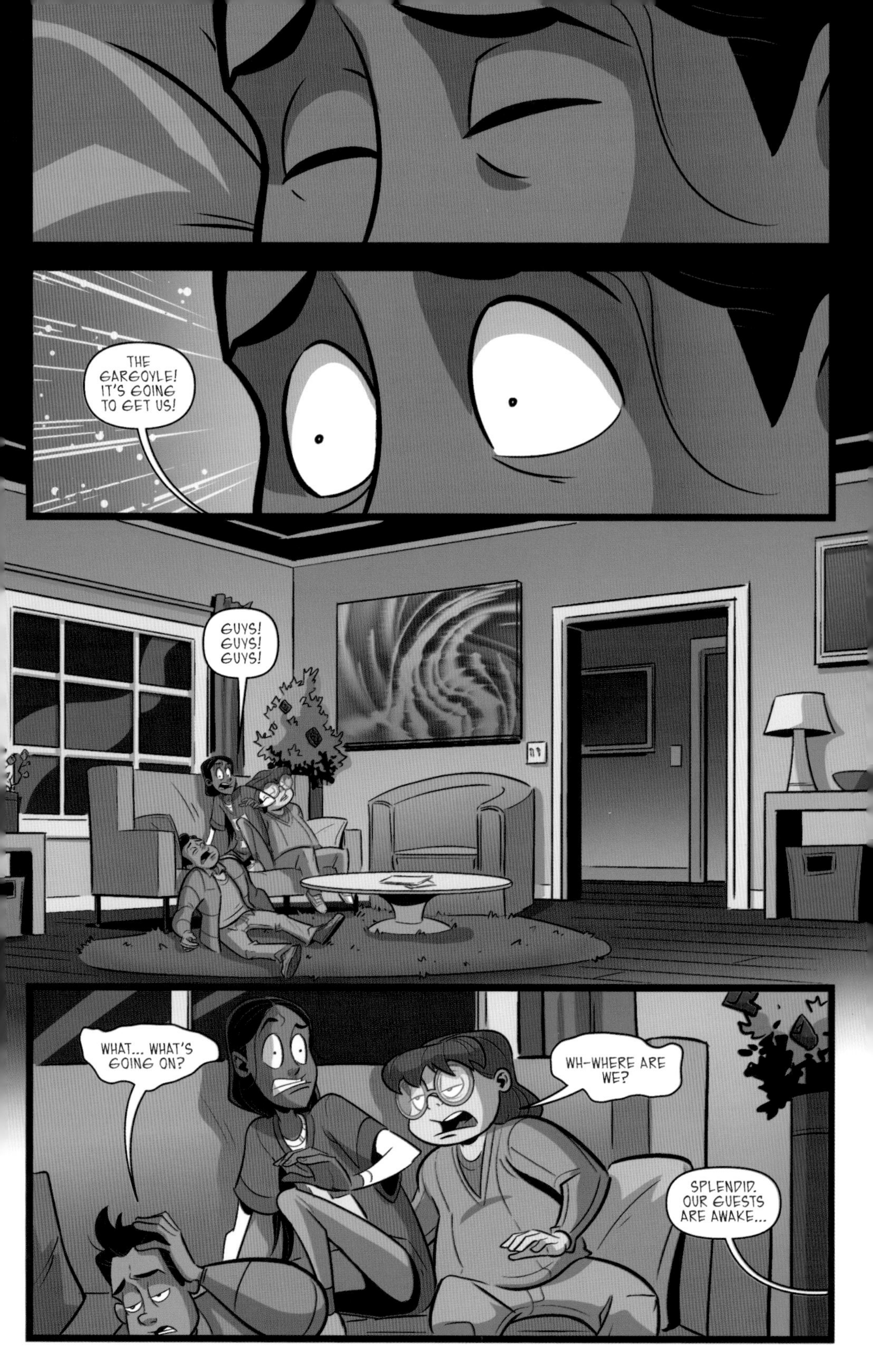
THE GARGOYLE! IT'S GOING TO GET US!
GUYS! GUYS! GUYS!
WHAT... WHAT'S GOING ON?
WH-WHERE ARE WE?
SPLENDID. OUR GUESTS ARE AWAKE...

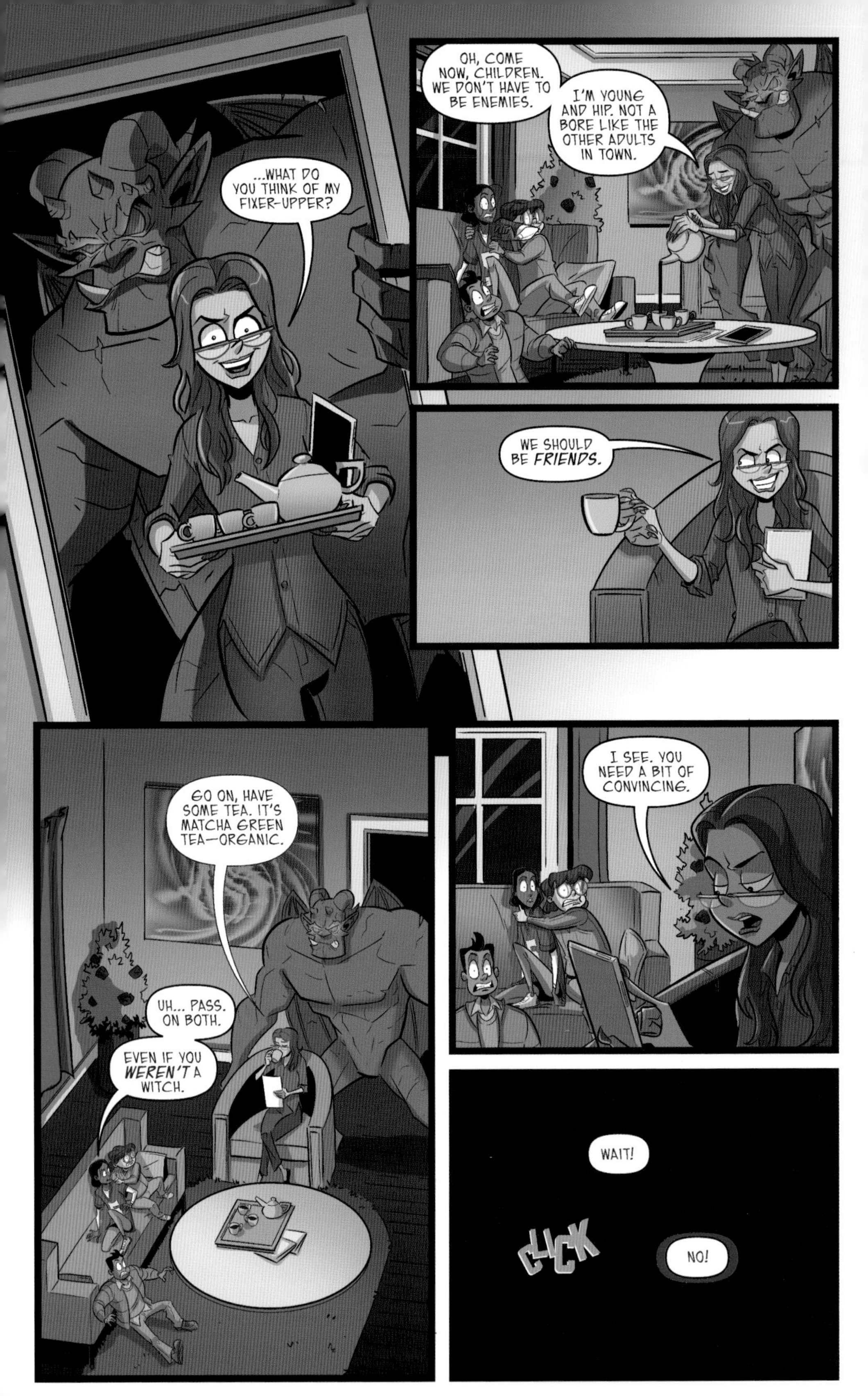
...WHAT DO YOU THINK OF MY FIXER-UPPER?
OH, COME NOW, CHILDREN. WE DON'T HAVE TO BE ENEMIES.
I'M YOUNG AND HIP. NOT A BORE LIKE THE OTHER ADULTS IN TOWN.
WE SHOULD BE *FRIENDS.*
GO ON, HAVE SOME TEA. IT'S MATCHA GREEN TEA—ORGANIC.
UH... PASS. ON BOTH.
EVEN IF YOU *WEREN'T* A WITCH.
I SEE. YOU NEED A BIT OF CONVINCING.
WAIT!
CLICK
NO!

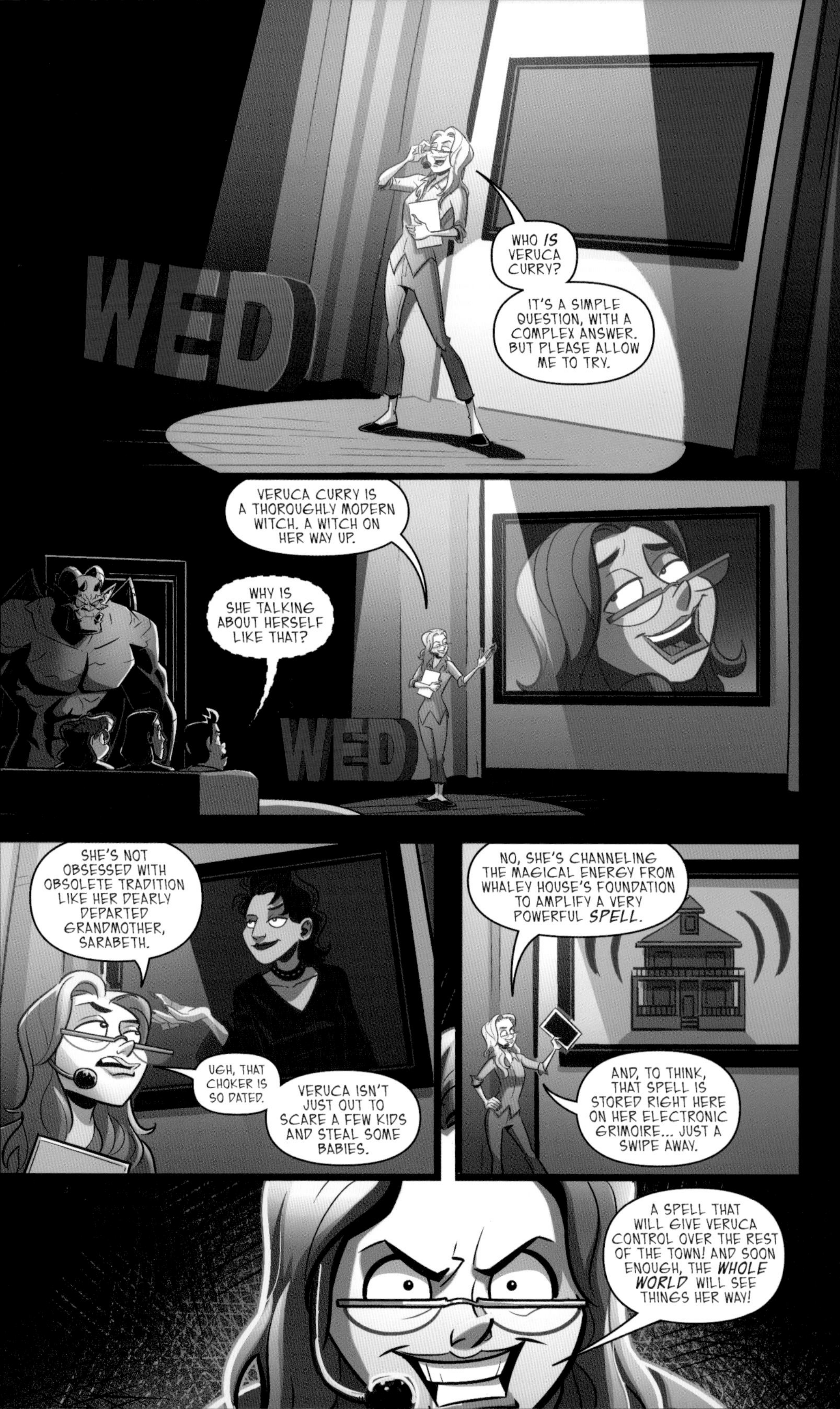

WHO IS VERUCA CURRY?
IT'S A SIMPLE QUESTION, WITH A COMPLEX ANSWER. BUT PLEASE ALLOW ME TO TRY.
WED
VERUCA CURRY IS A THOROUGHLY MODERN WITCH. A WITCH ON HER WAY UP.
WHY IS SHE TALKING ABOUT HERSELF LIKE THAT?
WED
SHE'S NOT OBSESSED WITH OBSOLETE TRADITION LIKE HER DEARLY DEPARTED GRANDMOTHER, SARABETH.
UGH, THAT CHOKER IS SO DATED.
VERUCA ISN'T JUST OUT TO SCARE A FEW KIDS AND STEAL SOME BABIES.
NO, SHE'S CHANNELING THE MAGICAL ENERGY FROM WHALEY HOUSE'S FOUNDATION TO AMPLIFY A VERY POWERFUL SPELL.
AND, TO THINK, THAT SPELL IS STORED RIGHT HERE ON HER ELECTRONIC GRIMOIRE... JUST A SWIPE AWAY.
A SPELL THAT WILL GIVE VERUCA CONTROL OVER THE REST OF THE TOWN! AND SOON ENOUGH, THE WHOLE WORLD WILL SEE THINGS HER WAY!

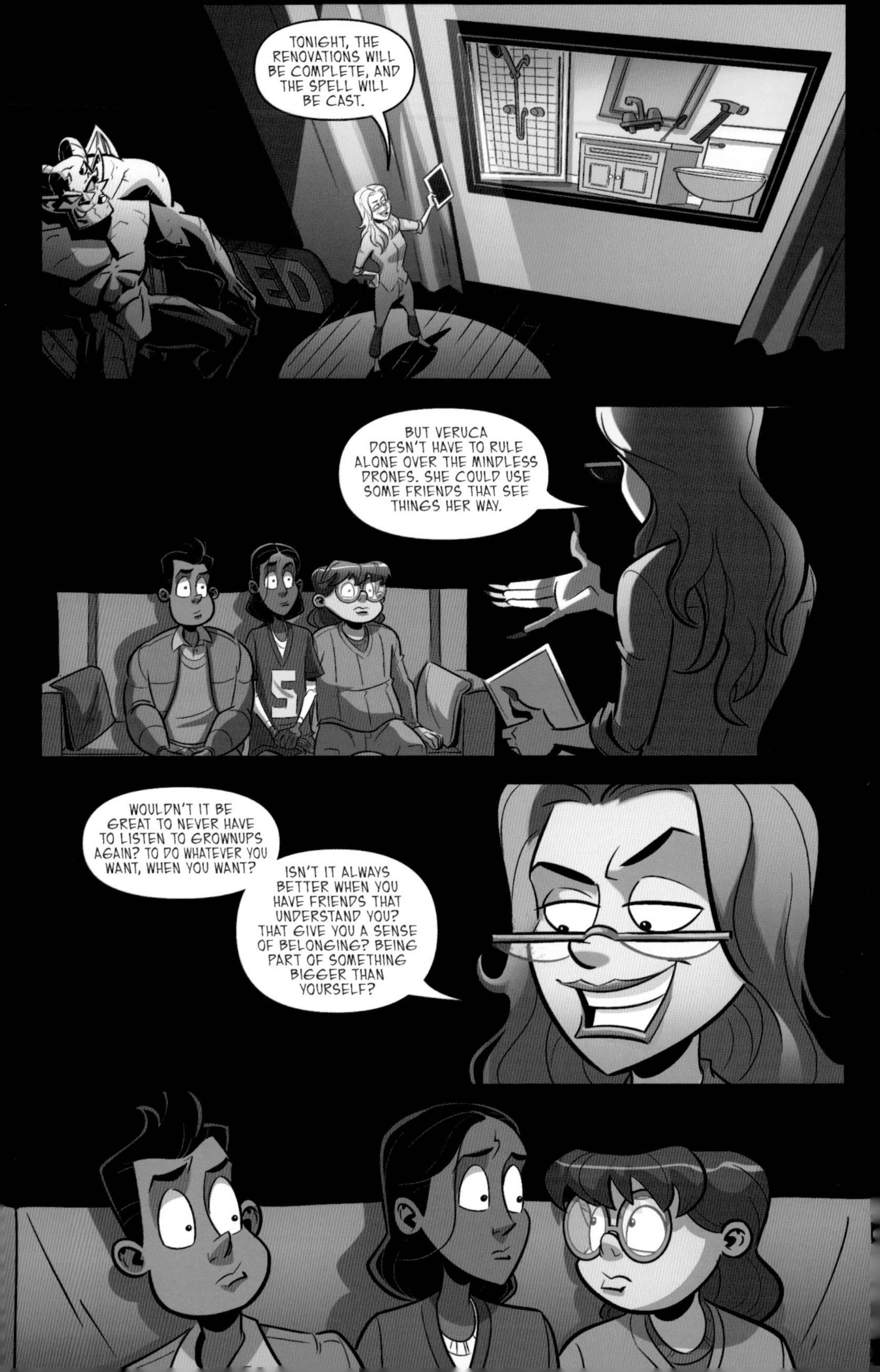
TONIGHT, THE RENOVATIONS WILL BE COMPLETE, AND THE SPELL WILL BE CAST.
BUT VERUCA DOESN'T HAVE TO RULE ALONE OVER THE MINDLESS DRONES. SHE COULD USE SOME FRIENDS THAT SEE THINGS HER WAY.
WOULDN'T IT BE GREAT TO NEVER HAVE TO LISTEN TO GROWNUPS AGAIN? TO DO WHATEVER YOU WANT, WHEN YOU WANT?
ISN'T IT ALWAYS BETTER WHEN YOU HAVE FRIENDS THAT UNDERSTAND YOU? THAT GIVE YOU A SENSE OF BELONGING? BEING PART OF SOMETHING BIGGER THAN YOURSELF?

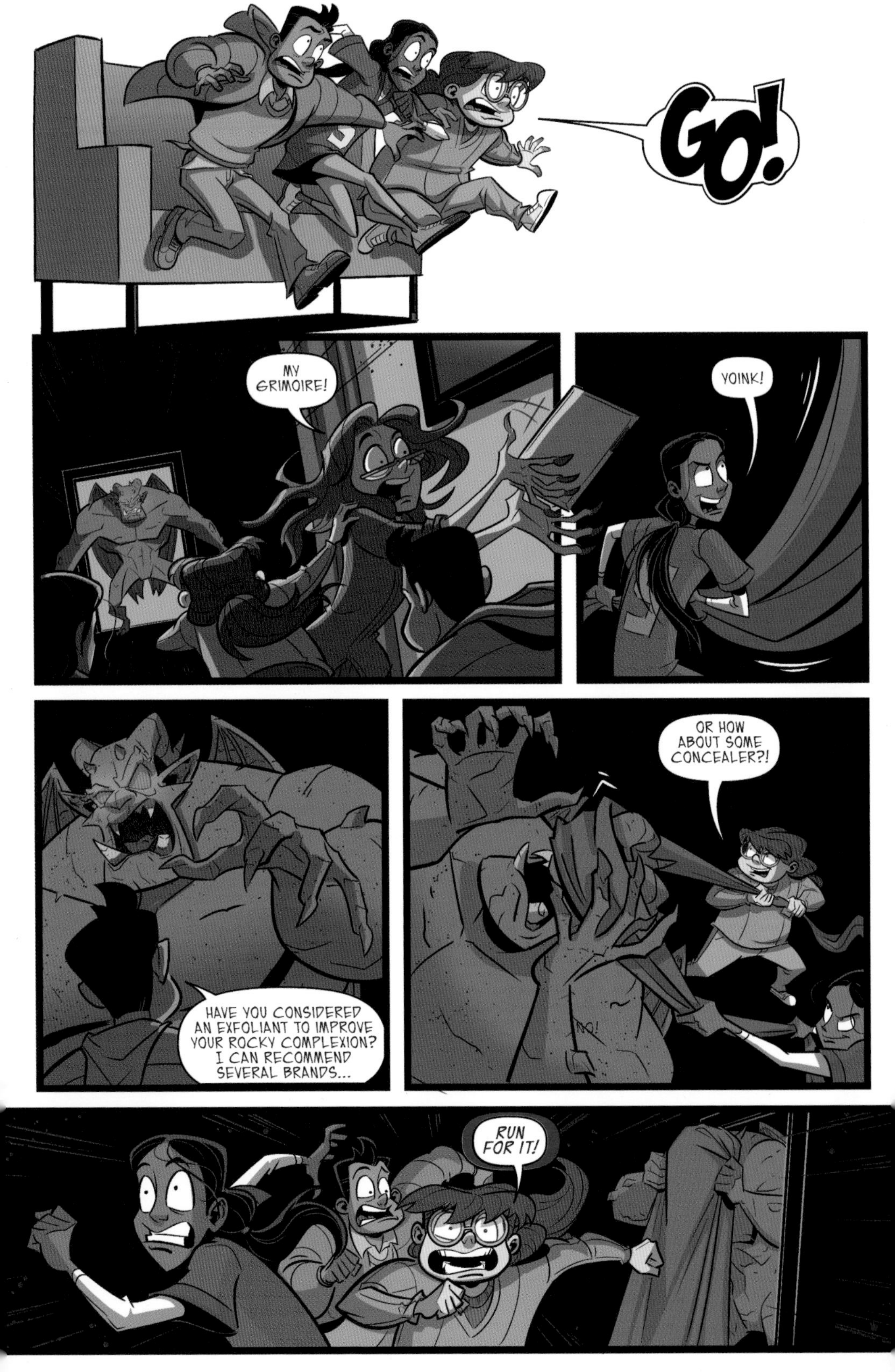
GO!
MY GRIMOIRE!
YOINK!
HAVE YOU CONSIDERED AN EXFOLIANT TO IMPROVE YOUR ROCKY COMPLEXION? I CAN RECOMMEND SEVERAL BRANDS...
OR HOW ABOUT SOME CONCEALER?!
RUN FOR IT!

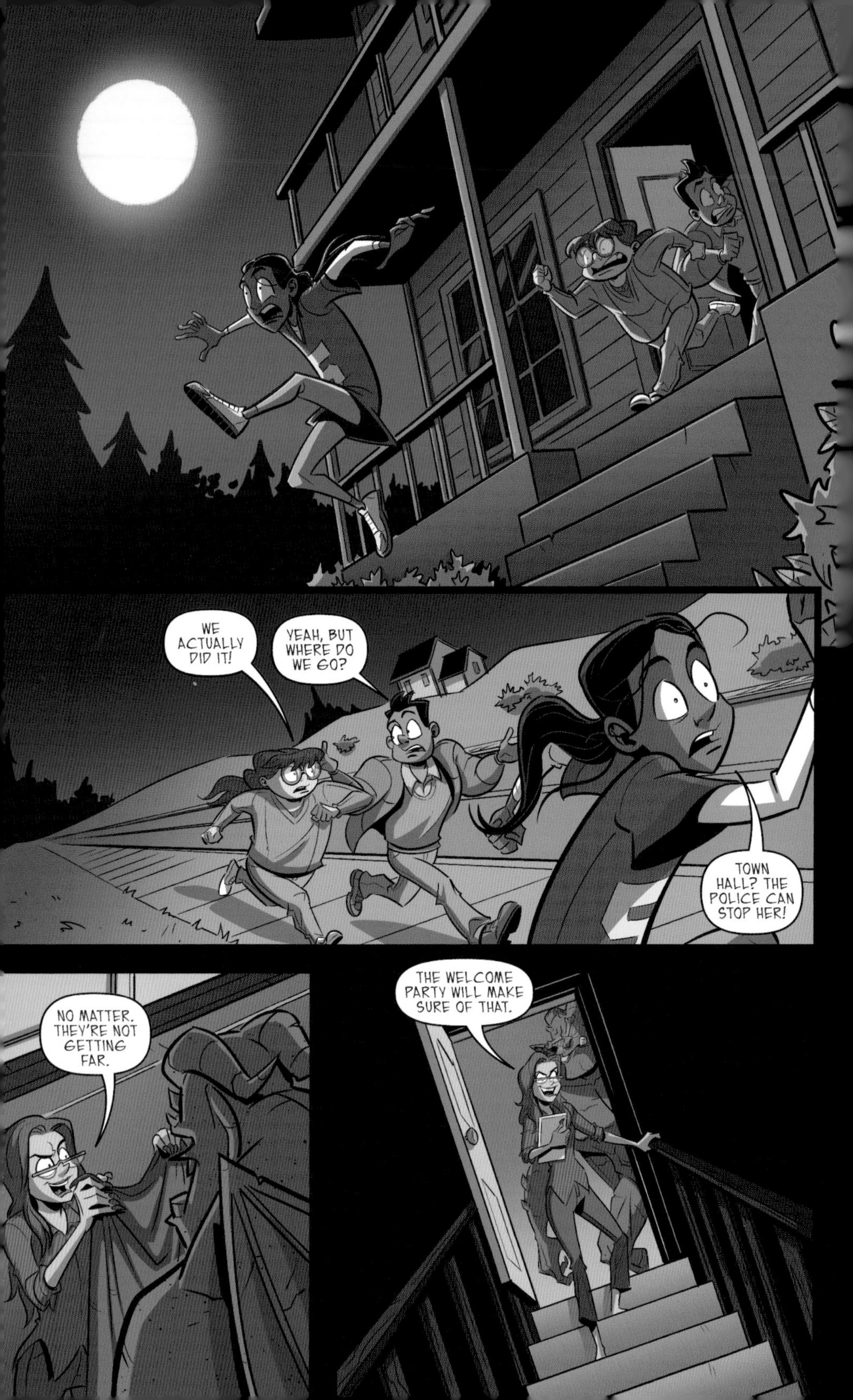
WE ACTUALLY DID IT!
YEAH, BUT WHERE DO WE GO?
TOWN HALL? THE POLICE CAN STOP HER!
NO MATTER. THEY'RE NOT GETTING FAR.
THE WELCOME PARTY WILL MAKE SURE OF THAT.

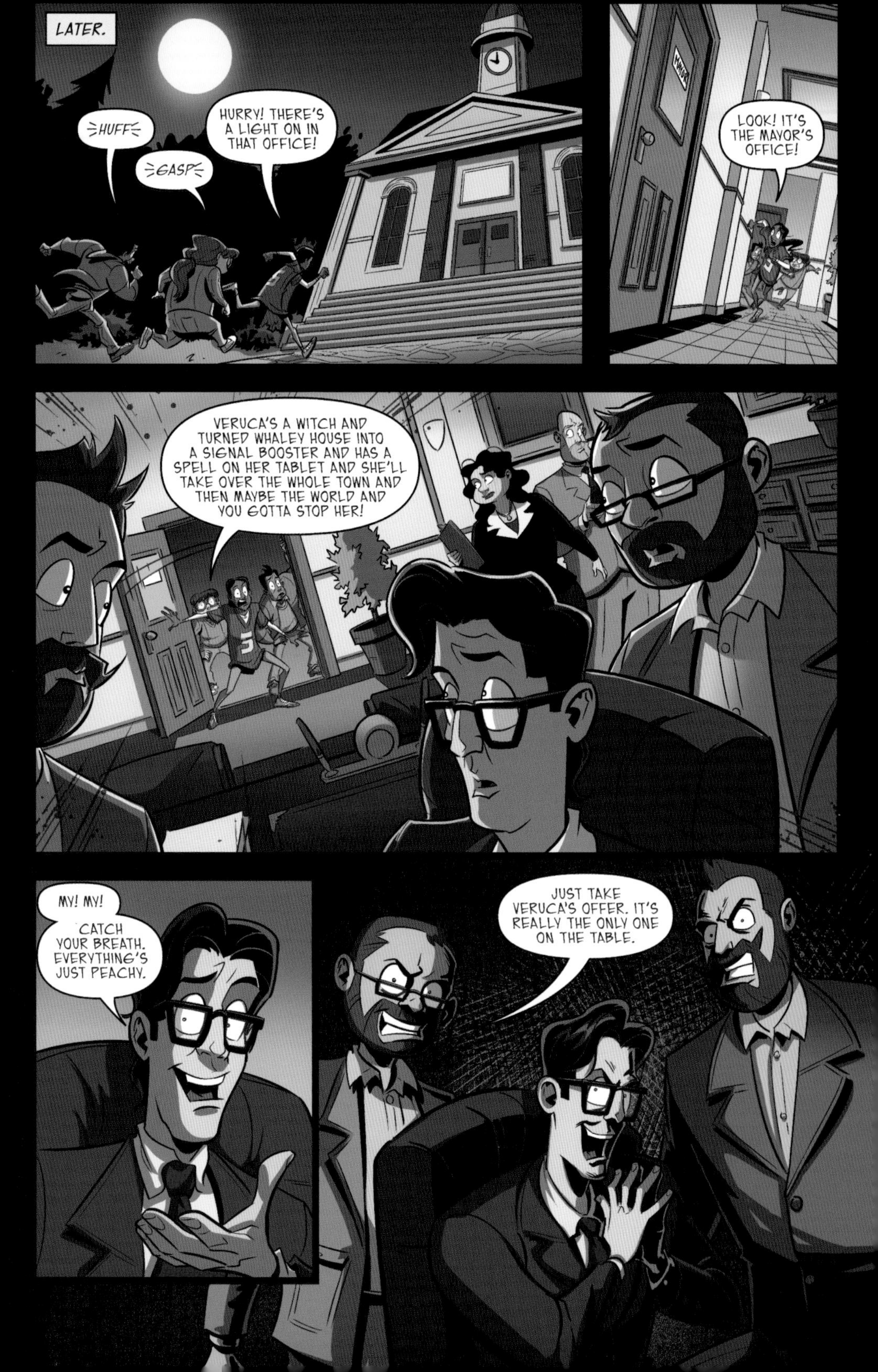
LATER.
HUFF
GASP
HURRY! THERE'S A LIGHT ON IN THAT OFFICE!
MAYOR
LOOK! IT'S THE MAYOR'S OFFICE!
VERUCA'S A WITCH AND TURNED WHALEY HOUSE INTO A SIGNAL BOOSTER AND HAS A SPELL ON HER TABLET AND SHE'LL TAKE OVER THE WHOLE TOWN AND THEN MAYBE THE WORLD AND YOU GOTTA STOP HER!
MY! MY!
CATCH YOUR BREATH. EVERYTHING'S JUST PEACHY.
JUST TAKE VERUCA'S OFFER. IT'S REALLY THE ONLY ONE ON THE TABLE.

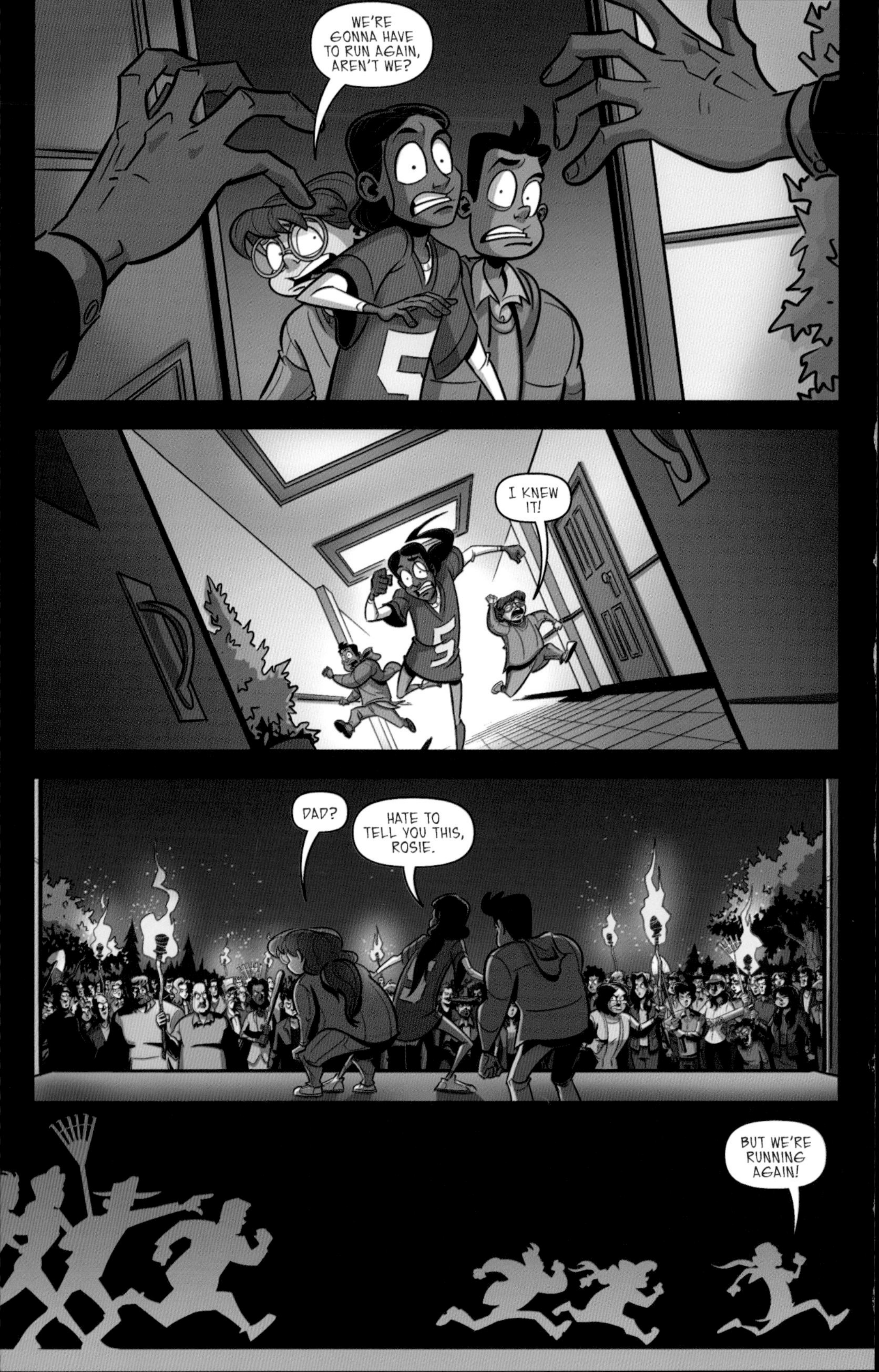
WE'RE GONNA HAVE TO RUN AGAIN, AREN'T WE?
I KNEW IT!
DAD?
HATE TO TELL YOU THIS, ROSIE.
BUT WE'RE RUNNING AGAIN!

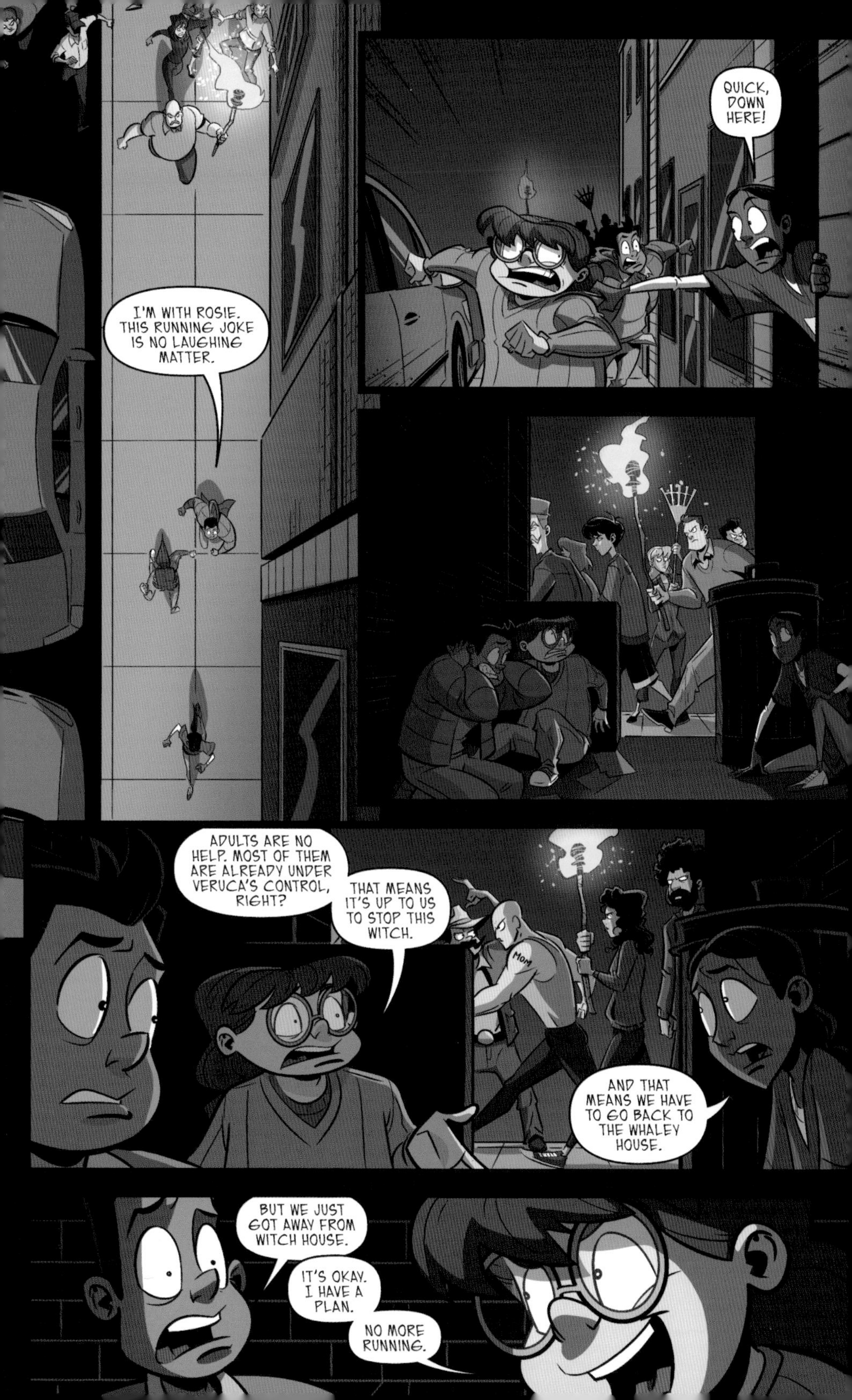
QUICK, DOWN HERE!
I'M WITH ROSIE. THIS RUNNING JOKE IS NO LAUGHING MATTER.
ADULTS ARE NO HELP. MOST OF THEM ARE ALREADY UNDER VERUCA'S CONTROL, RIGHT?
THAT MEANS IT'S UP TO US TO STOP THIS WITCH.
MOM
AND THAT MEANS WE HAVE TO GO BACK TO THE WHALEY HOUSE.
BUT WE JUST GOT AWAY FROM WITCH HOUSE.
IT'S OKAY. I HAVE A PLAN.
NO MORE RUNNING.

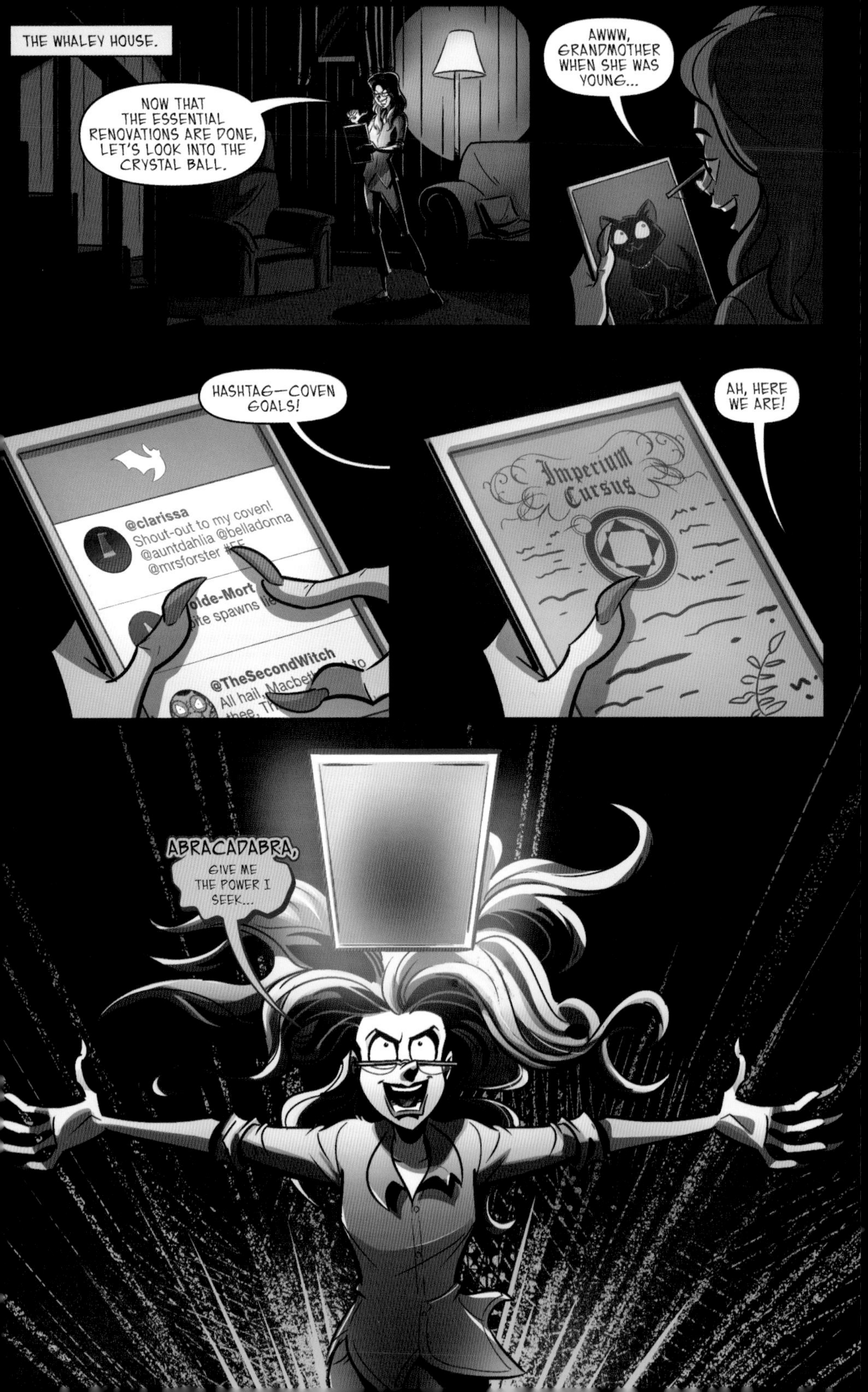
THE WHALEY HOUSE.
NOW THAT THE ESSENTIAL RENOVATIONS ARE DONE, LET'S LOOK INTO THE CRYSTAL BALL.
AWWW, GRANDMOTHER WHEN SHE WAS YOUNG...
HASHTAG—COVEN GOALS!
@clarissa
Shout-out to my coven! @auntdahlia @belladonna
@mrsforster #FF
@TheSecondWitch
AH, HERE WE ARE!
Imperium Cursus
ABRACADABRA,
GIVE ME THE POWER I SEEK...

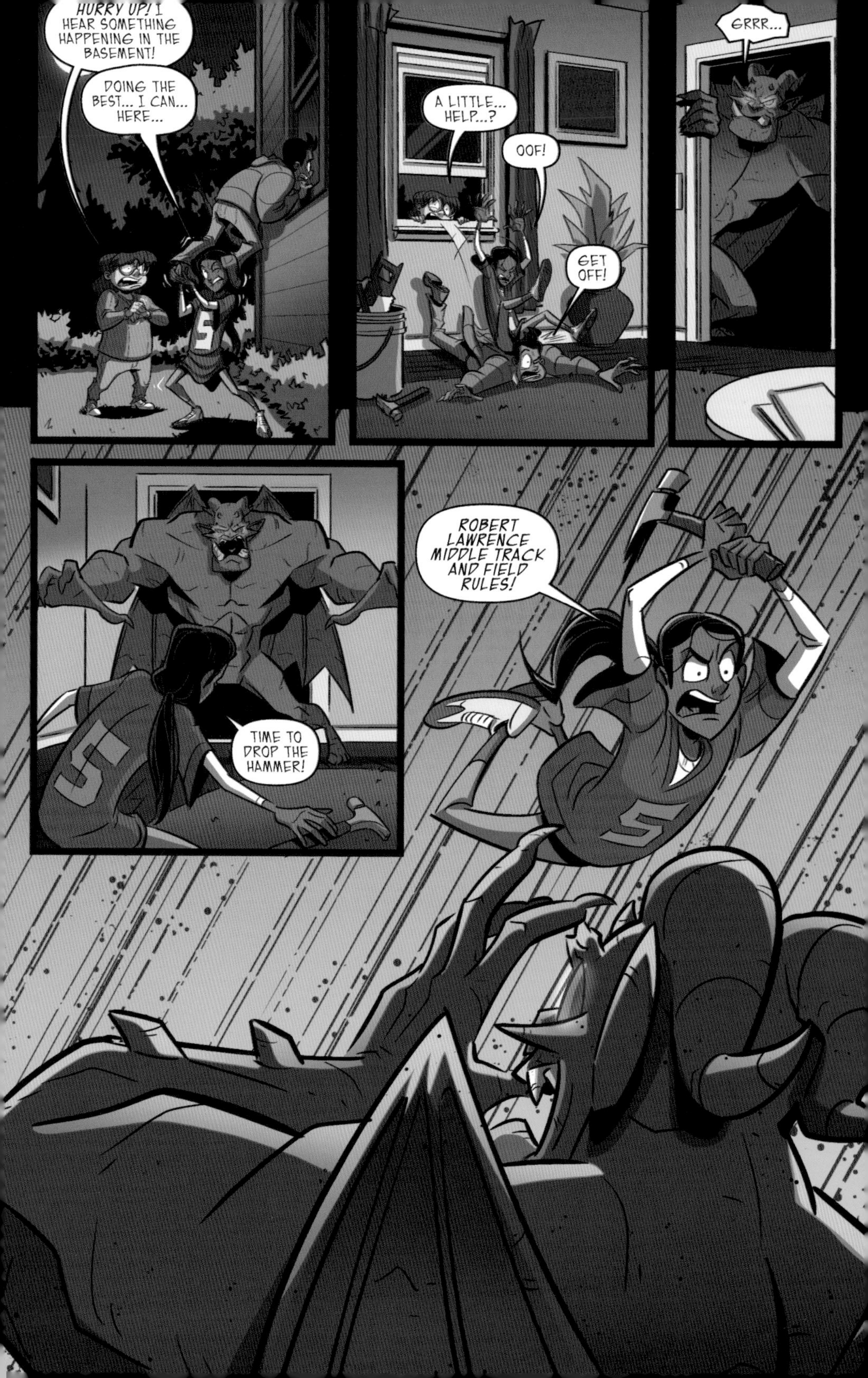
HURRY UP! I HEAR SOMETHING HAPPENING IN THE BASEMENT!
DOING THE BEST... I CAN... HERE...
A LITTLE... HELP...?
OOF!
GET OFF!
GRRR...
TIME TO DROP THE HAMMER!
ROBERT LAWRENCE MIDDLE TRACK AND FIELD RULES!

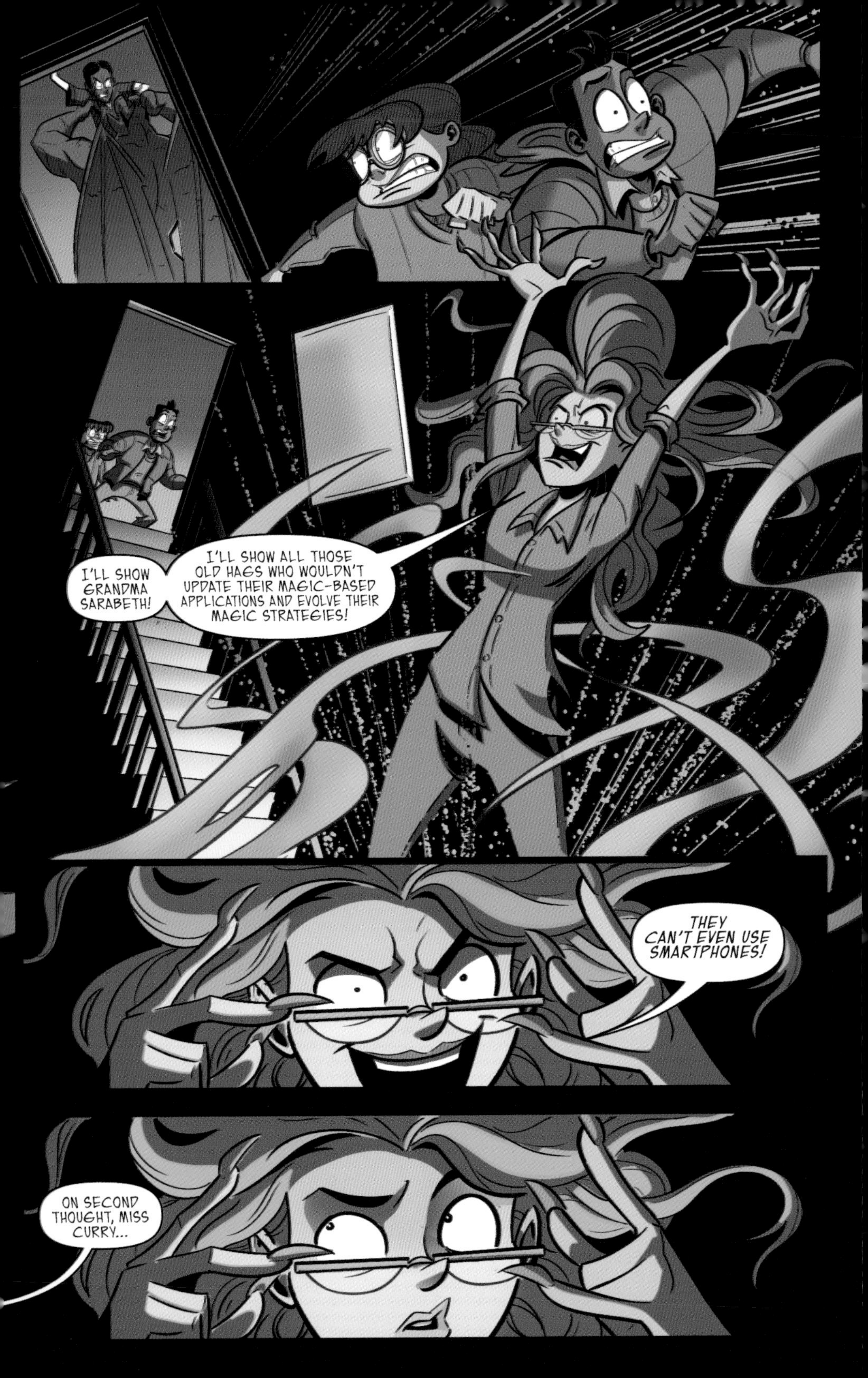
I'LL SHOW GRANDMA SARABETH!
I'LL SHOW ALL THOSE OLD HAGS WHO WOULDN'T UPDATE THEIR MAGIC-BASED APPLICATIONS AND EVOLVE THEIR MAGIC STRATEGIES!
THEY CAN'T EVEN USE SMARTPHONES!
ON SECOND THOUGHT, MISS CURRY...

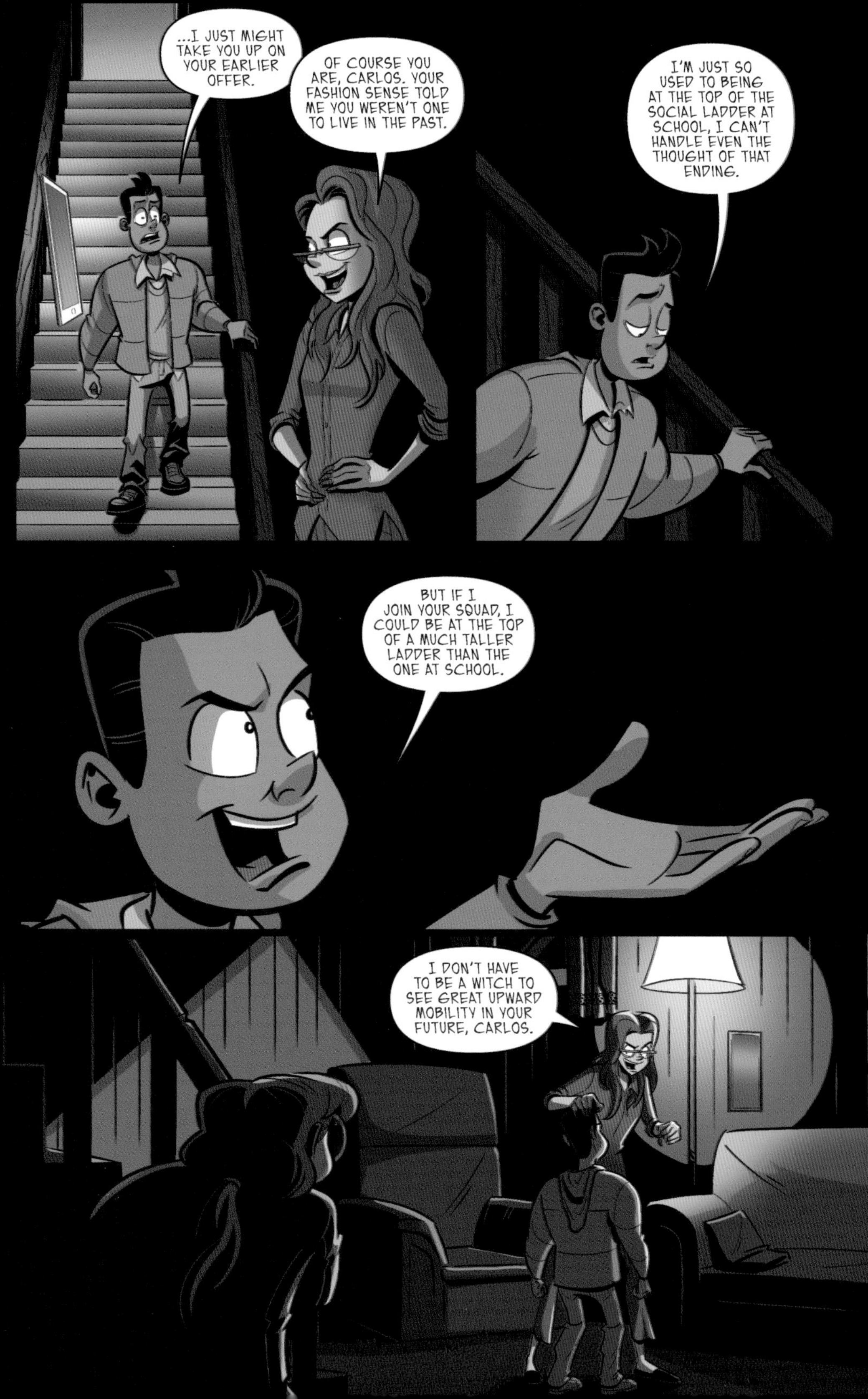
...I JUST MIGHT TAKE YOU UP ON YOUR EARLIER OFFER.
OF COURSE YOU ARE, CARLOS. YOUR FASHION SENSE TOLD ME YOU WEREN'T ONE TO LIVE IN THE PAST.
I'M JUST SO USED TO BEING AT THE TOP OF THE SOCIAL LADDER AT SCHOOL, I CAN'T HANDLE EVEN THE THOUGHT OF THAT ENDING.
BUT IF I JOIN YOUR SQUAD, I COULD BE AT THE TOP OF A MUCH TALLER LADDER THAN THE ONE AT SCHOOL.
I DON'T HAVE TO BE A WITCH TO SEE GREAT UPWARD MOBILITY IN YOUR FUTURE, CARLOS.

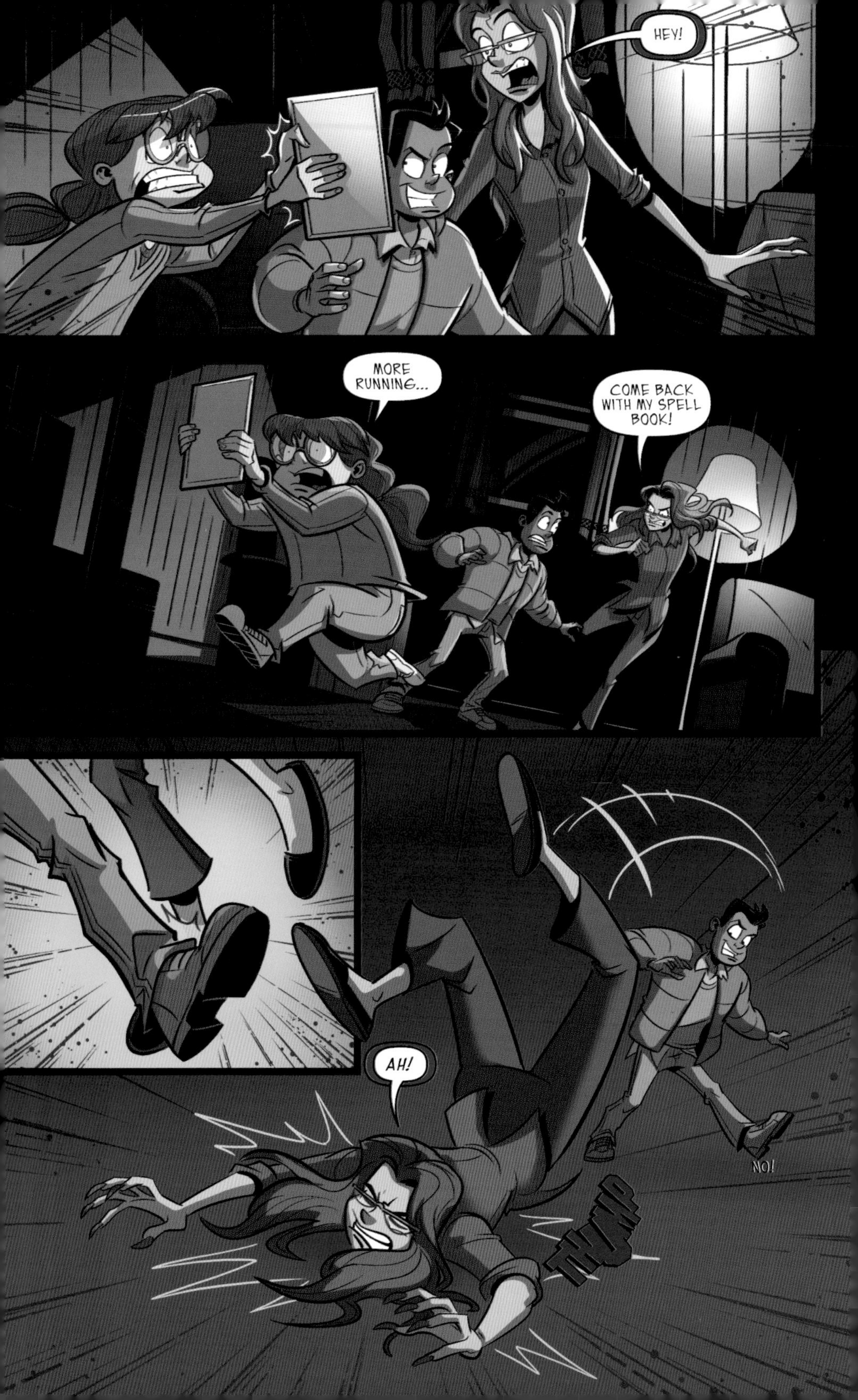
HEY!
MORE RUNNING...
COME BACK WITH MY SPELL BOOK!
AH!
THUMP
NO!

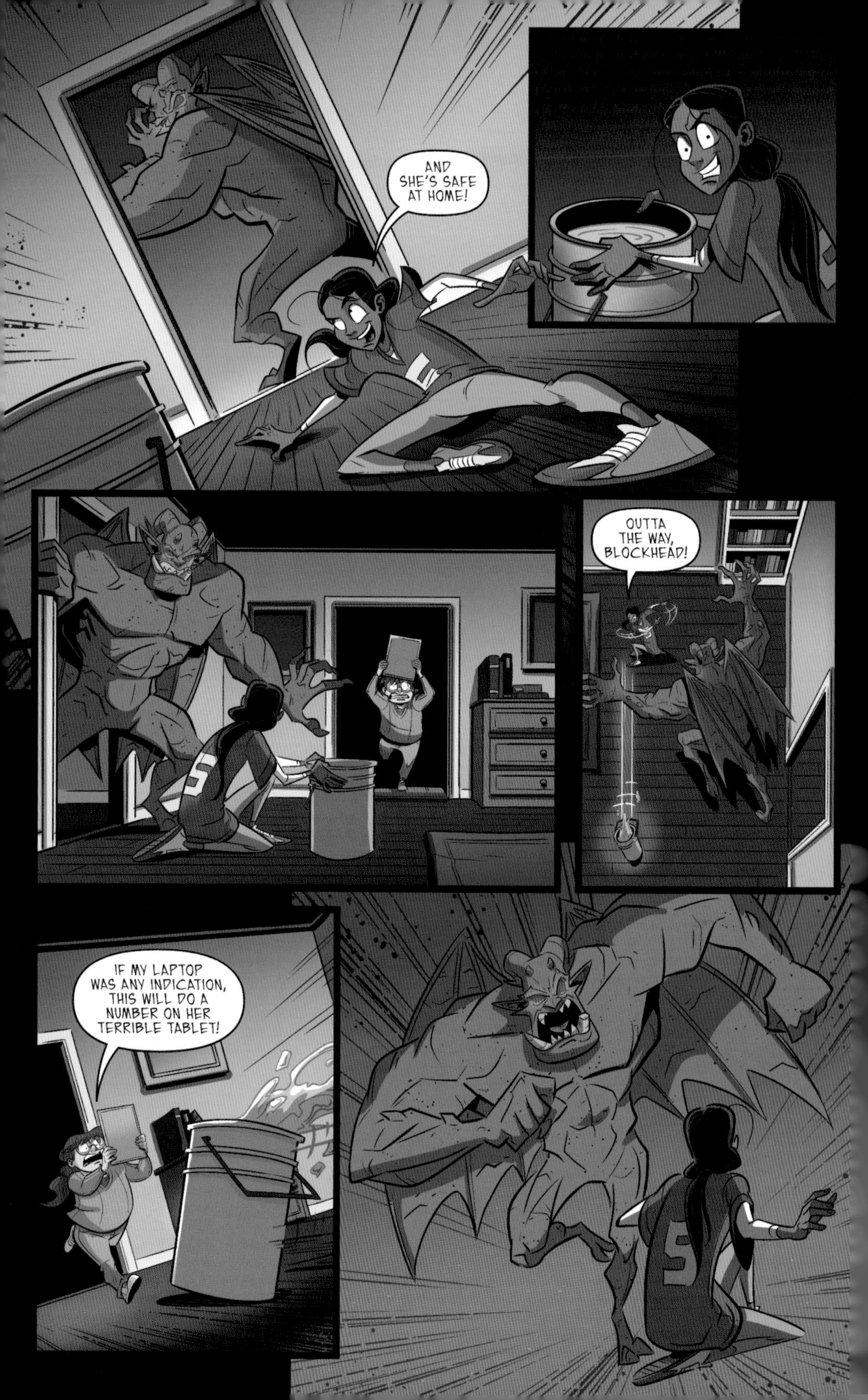
AND SHE'S SAFE AT HOME!
OUTTA THE WAY, BLOCKHEAD!
IF MY LAPTOP WAS ANY INDICATION, THIS WILL DO A NUMBER ON HER TERRIBLE TABLET!

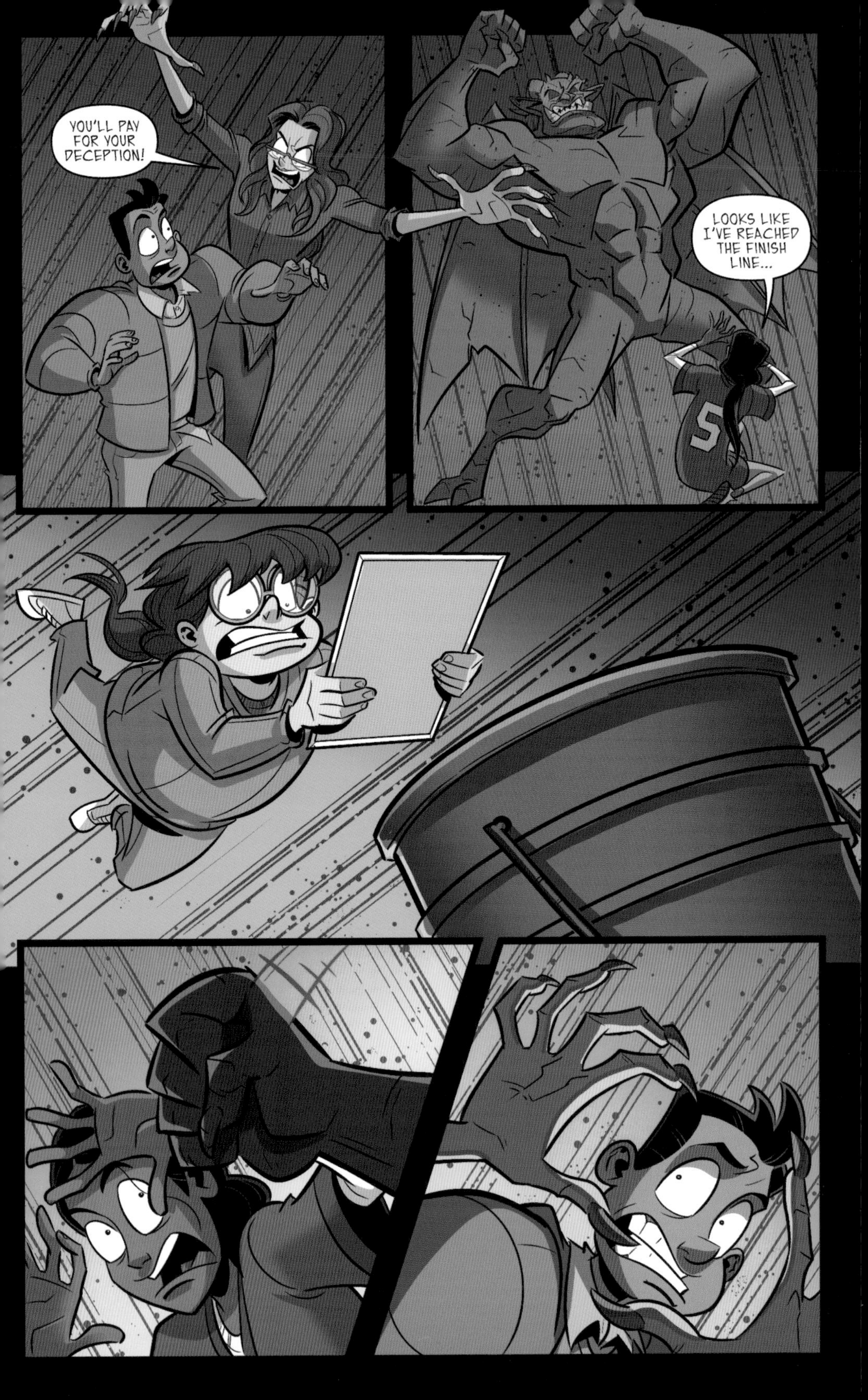
YOU'LL PAY FOR YOUR DECEPTION!
LOOKS LIKE I'VE REACHED THE FINISH LINE...
5

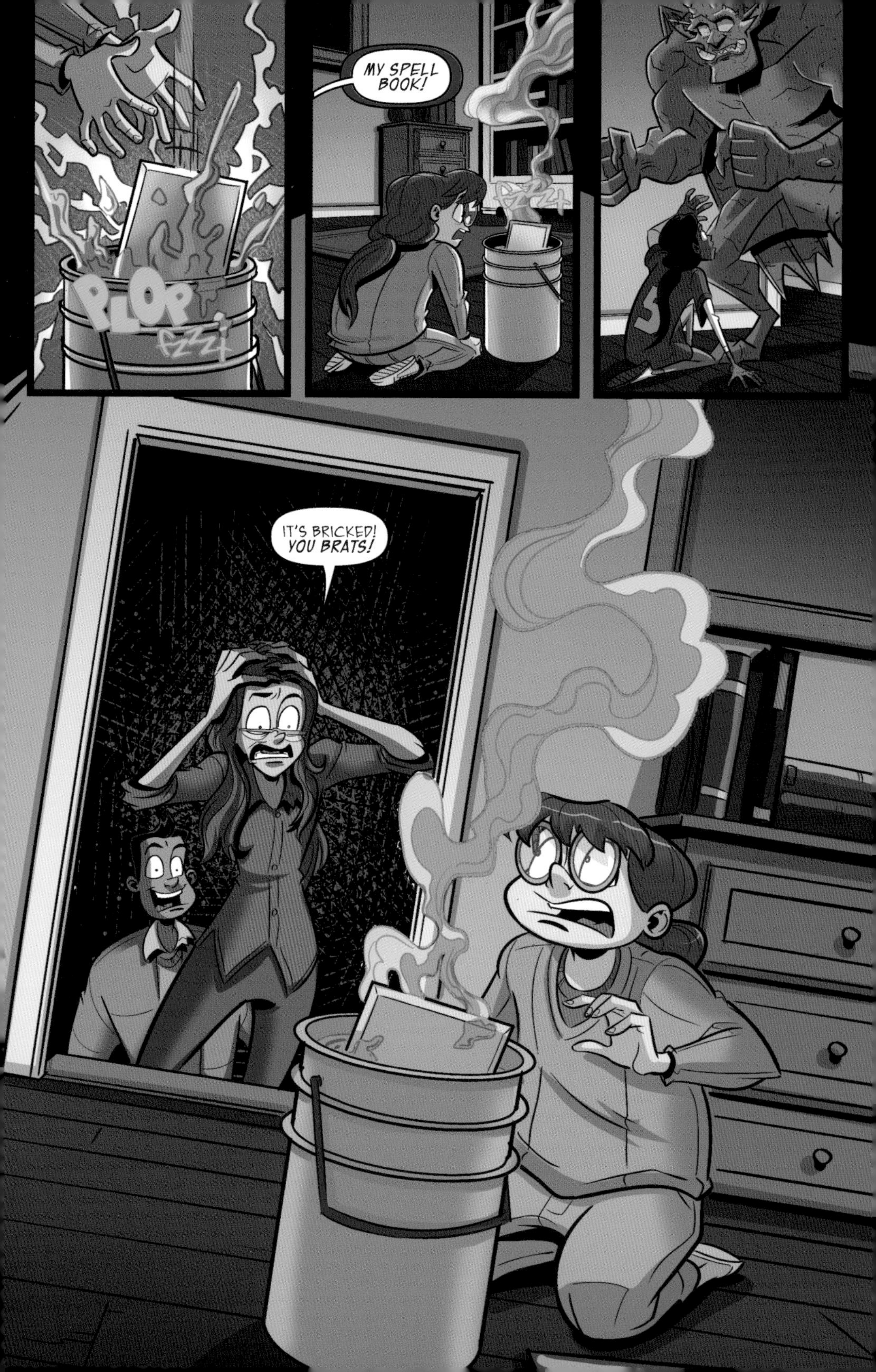
PLOP
fzzzt
MY SPELL BOOK!
fzzzt
IT'S BRICKED! YOU BRATS!

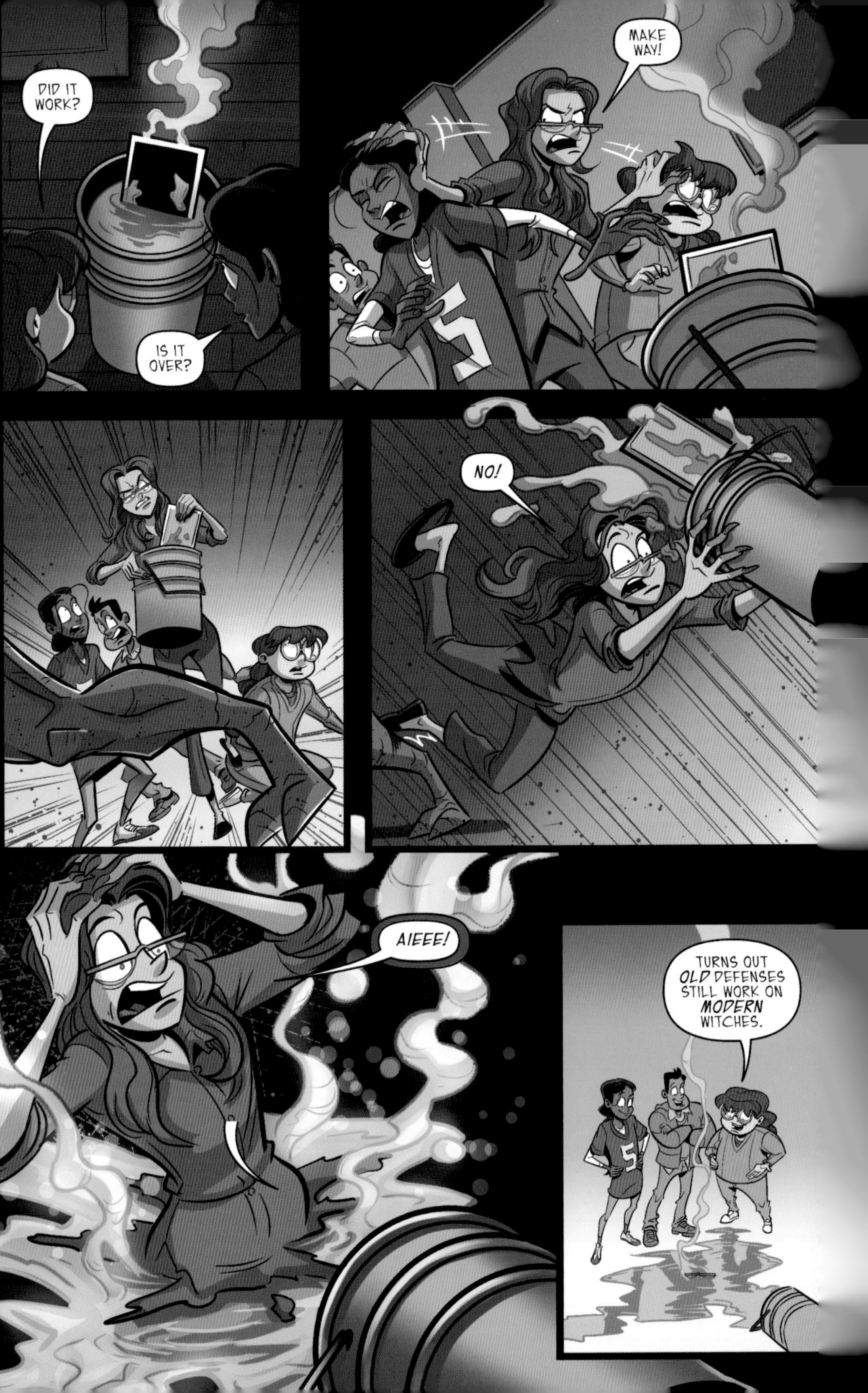
DID IT WORK?
IS IT OVER?
MAKE WAY!
NO!
AIEEE!
TURNS OUT OLD DEFENSES STILL WORK ON MODERN WITCHES.

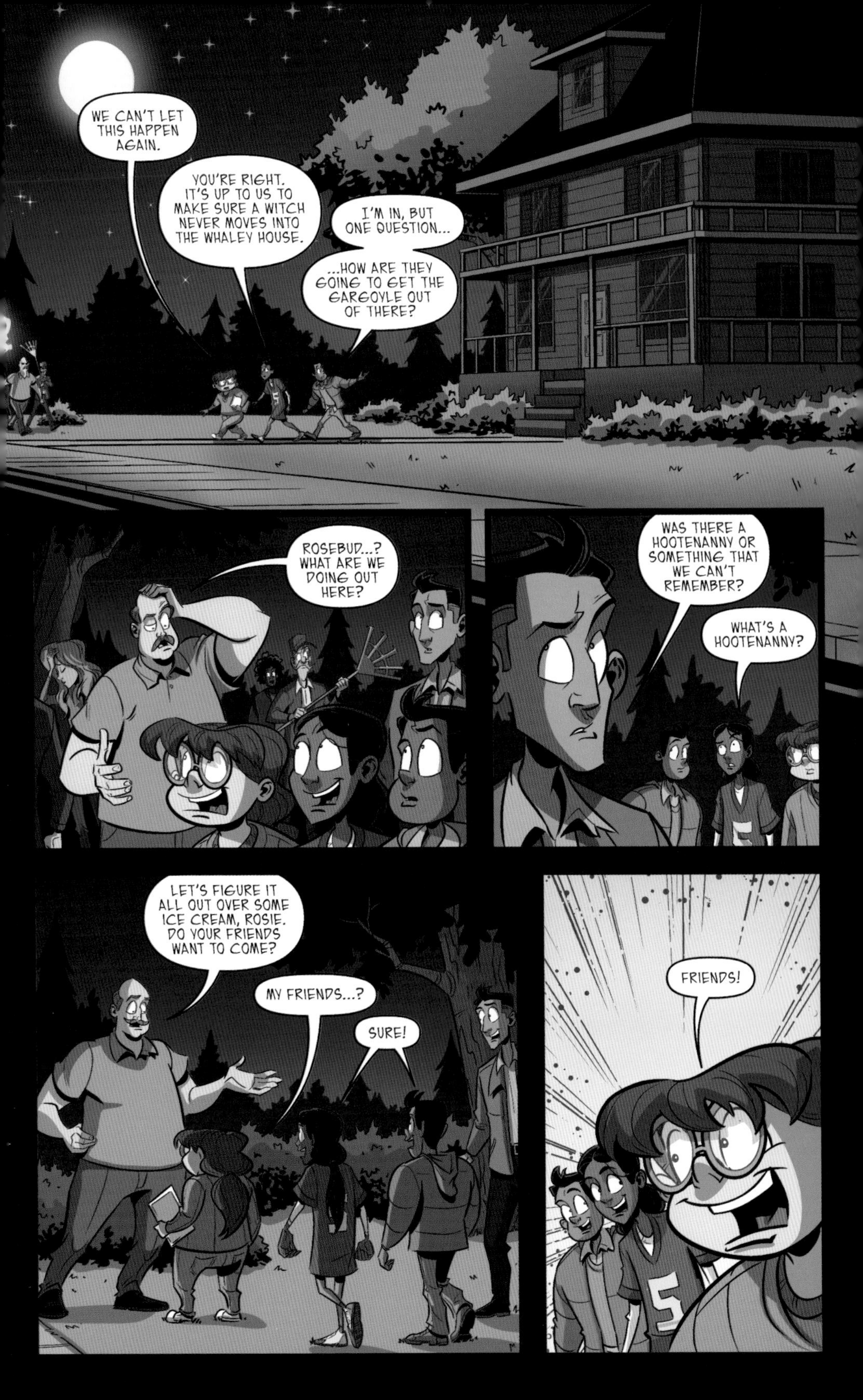
WE CAN'T LET THIS HAPPEN AGAIN.
YOU'RE RIGHT. IT'S UP TO US TO MAKE SURE A WITCH NEVER MOVES INTO THE WHALEY HOUSE.
I'M IN, BUT ONE QUESTION...
...HOW ARE THEY GOING TO GET THE GARGOYLE OUT OF THERE?
ROSEBUD...? WHAT ARE WE DOING OUT HERE?
WAS THERE A HOOTENANNY OR SOMETHING THAT WE CAN'T REMEMBER?
WHAT'S A HOOTENANNY?
LET'S FIGURE IT ALL OUT OVER SOME ICE CREAM, ROSIE. DO YOUR FRIENDS WANT TO COME?
MY FRIENDS...?
SURE!
FRIENDS!

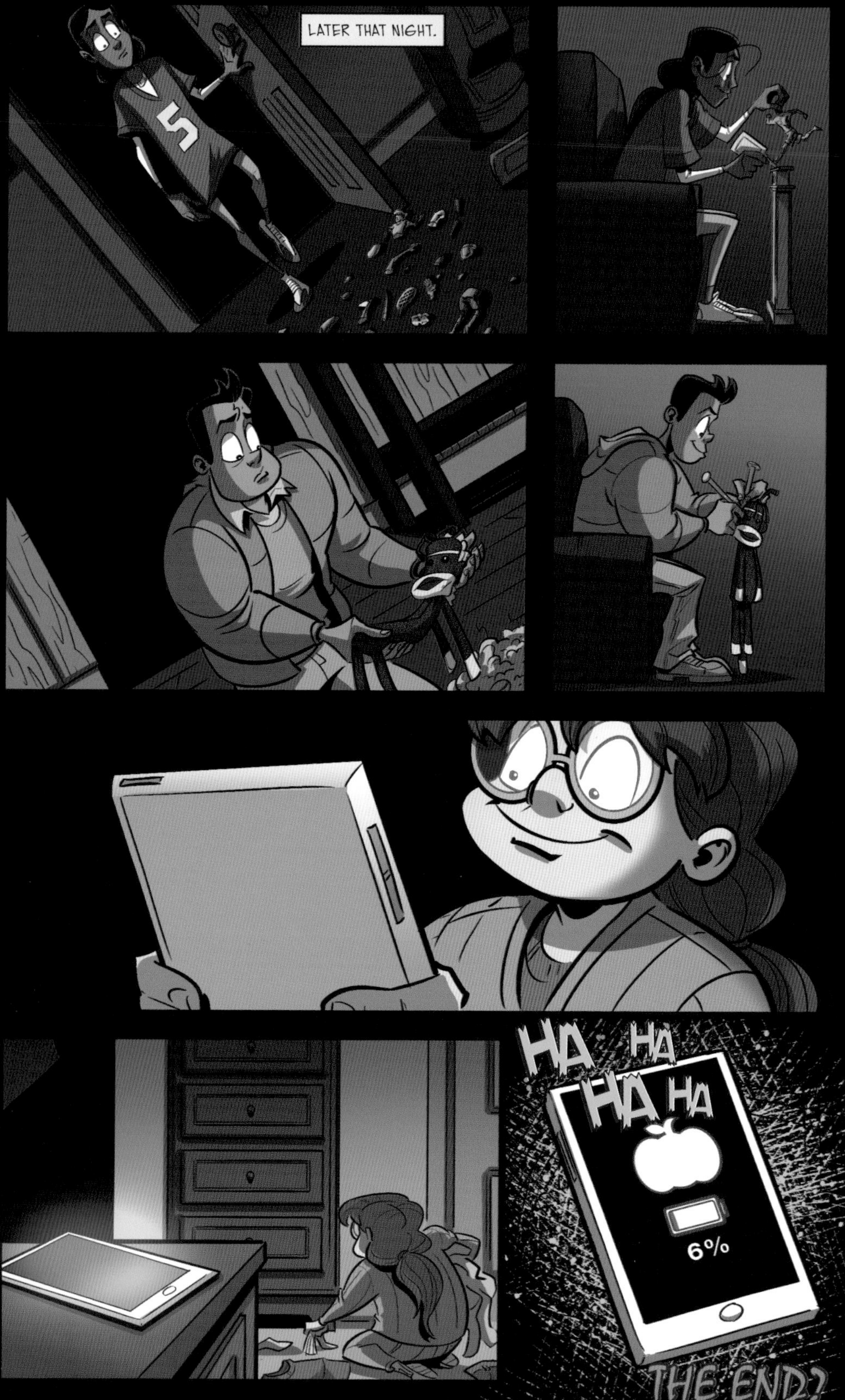
LATER THAT NIGHT.
HA HA
HA HA
6%
THE END?

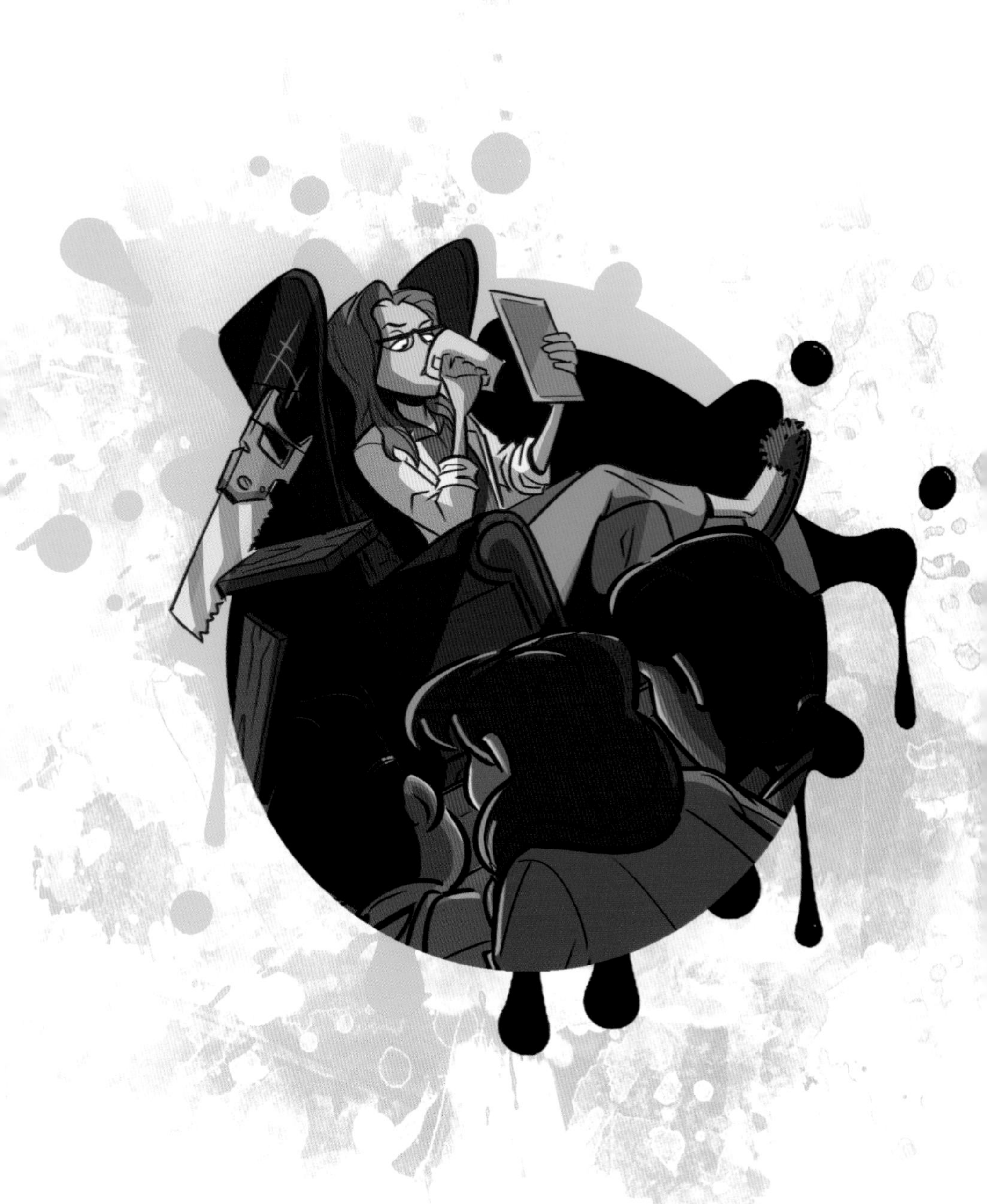

ART BY **MEGAN LEVENS**
COLORS BY **LEONARDO ITO**

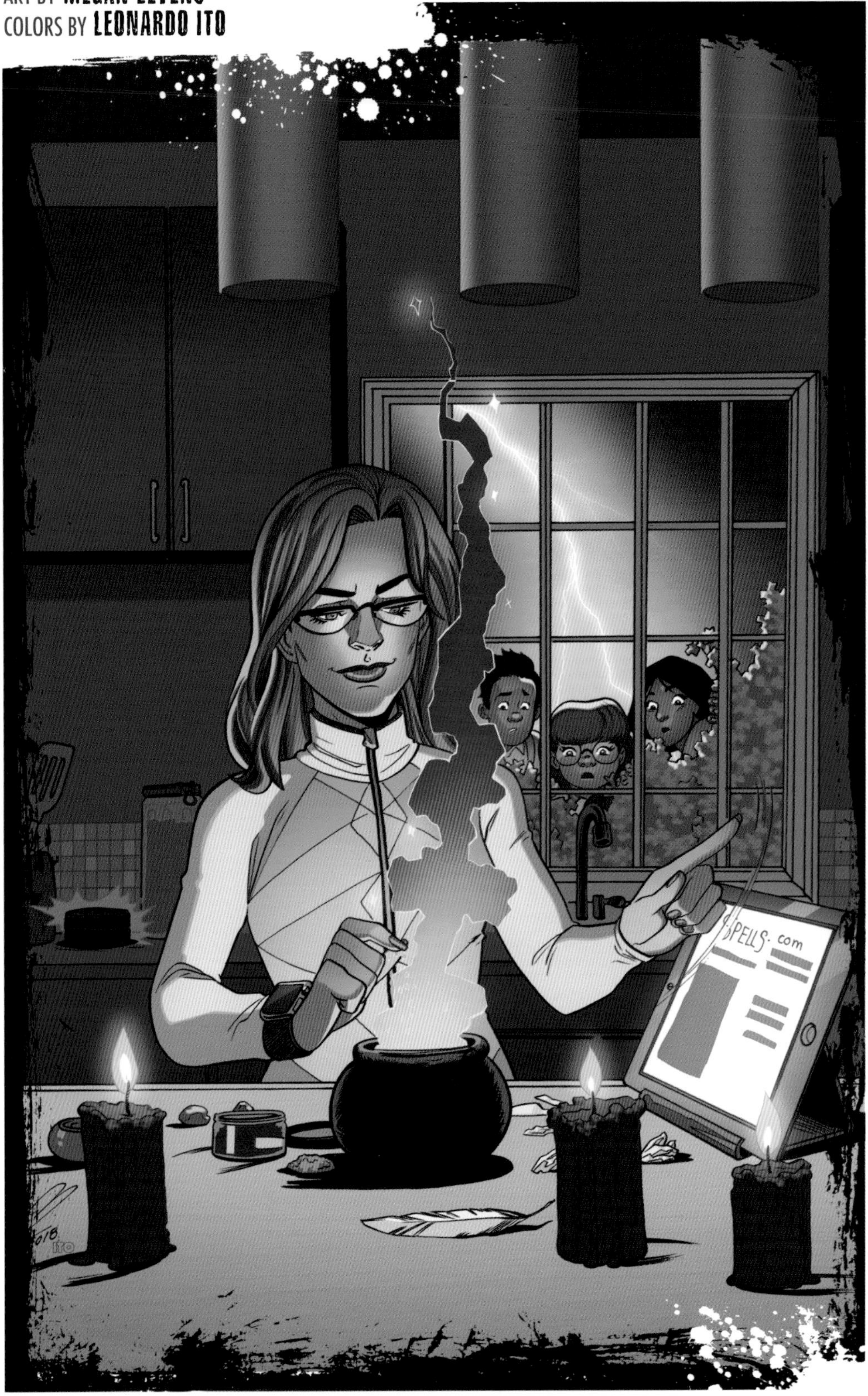
SPELLS.com

ART BY **MEGAN LEVENS**
COLORS BY **LEONARDO ITO**

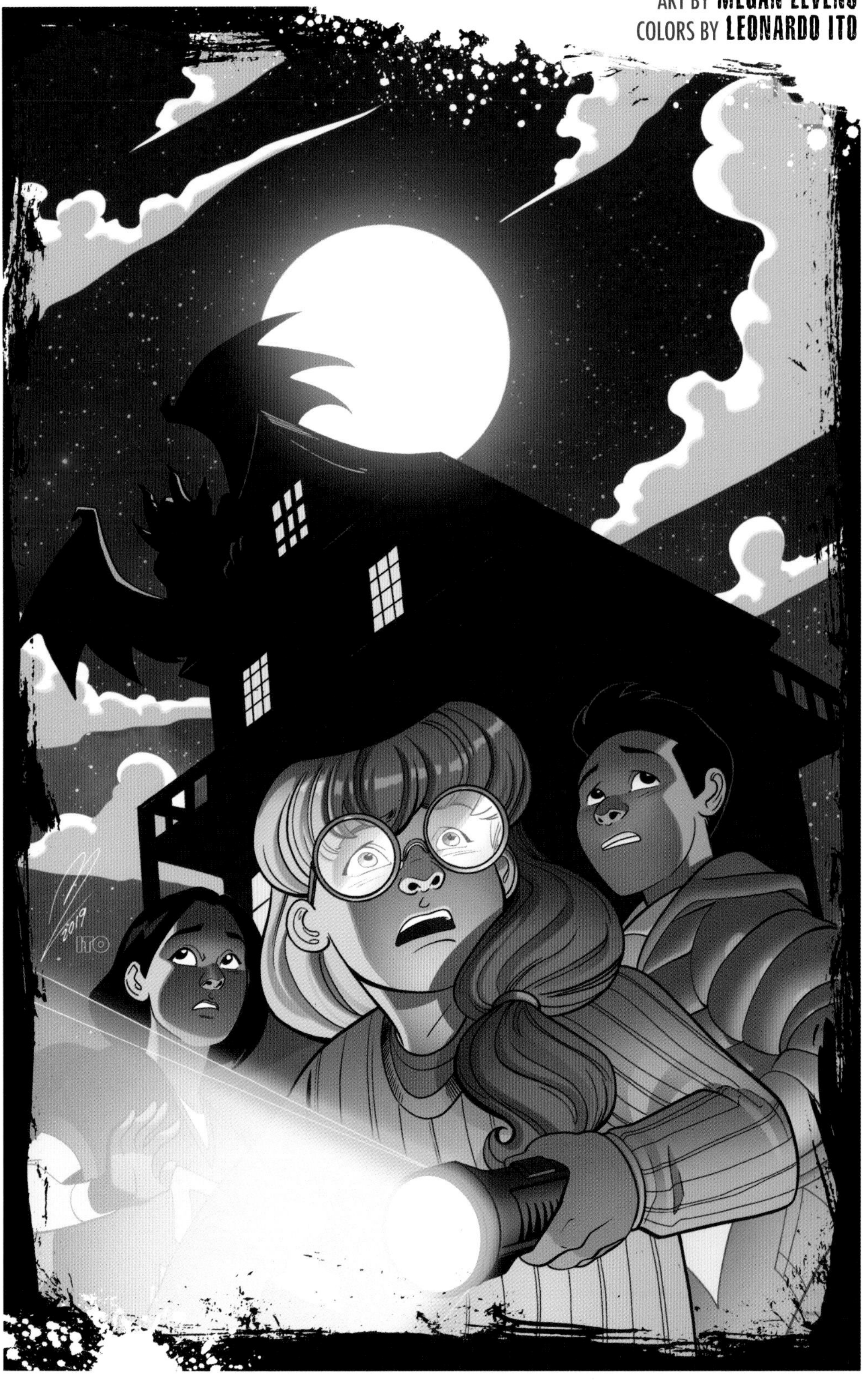
2019
ITO

ART BY MEGAN LEVENS
COLORS BY LEONARDO ITO

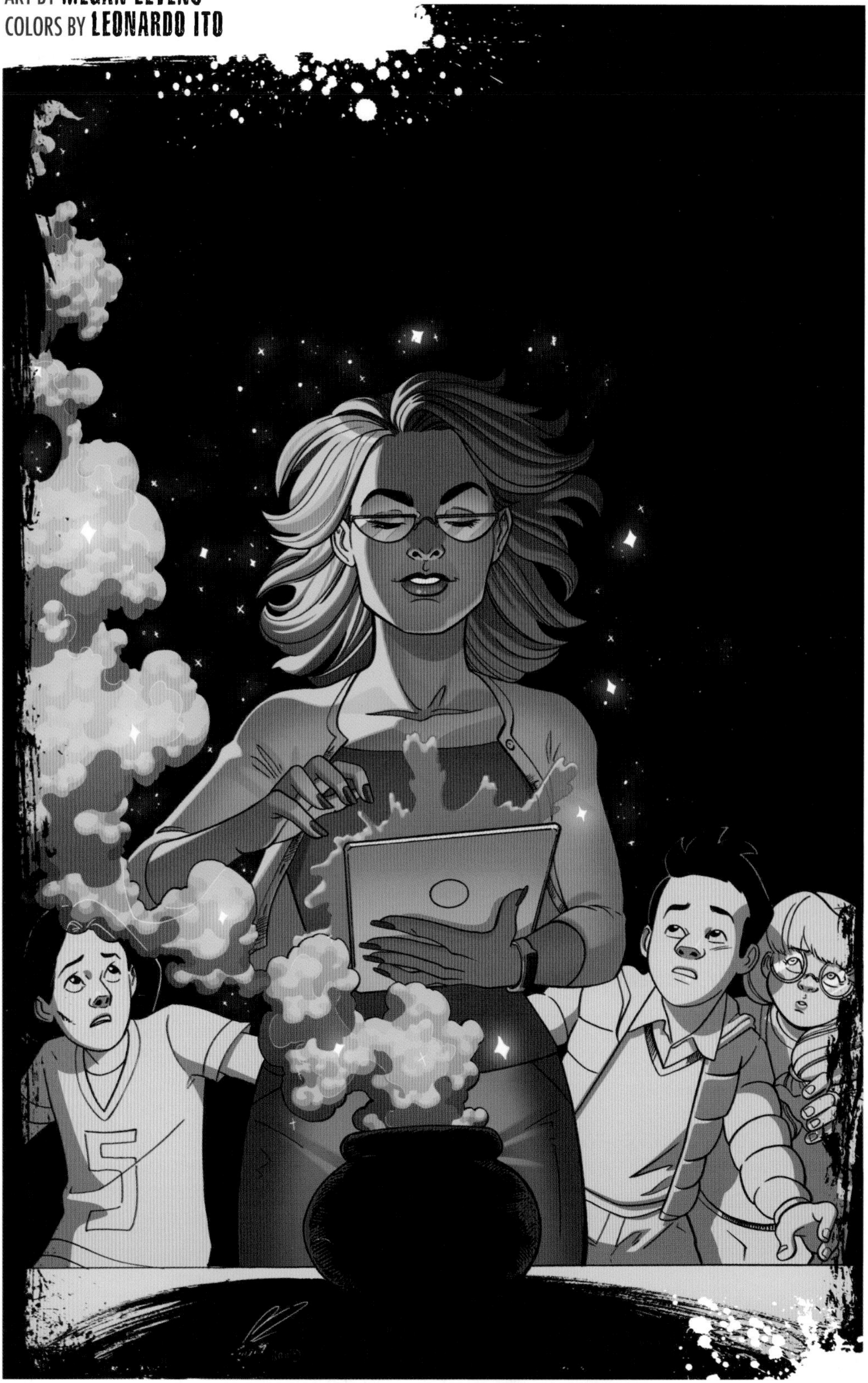